## What was happening

First someone tried to kill her underwater, now her home was ransacked.

"Go get cleaned up," Shep said as he surveyed the disaster.

Right now Caley didn't need clean clothes. What she needed was comfort.

Shep had proven he could protect her physically. But she needed emotional security and that wasn't his strong suit.

Still, she inched toward him, and he backed up until the counter blocked his getaway.

She slipped her arms around him and rested her head on his chest. "I know this isn't part of your assignment, but I need a hug. I need you to tell me everything's going to be fine."

Slowly his arms encircled her. "Everything will." His voice faltered but held enough confidence she believed him. His chest felt like an iron wall that no one could penetrate. Sheltered by him, no one could touch her. And while that brought comfort, it was also terrifying.

At some point Shep would let go. But whoever was after her wouldn't stop. Not until he had what he wanted...or she was dead.

**Jessica R. Patch** lives in the mid-South, where she pens inspirational contemporary romance and romantic suspense novels. When she's not hunched over her laptop or going on adventurous trips with willing friends in the name of research, you can find her watching way too much Netflix with her family and collecting recipes to amazing dishes she'll probably never cook. To learn more about Jessica, please visit her at jessicarpatch.com.

### Books by Jessica R. Patch

### Love Inspired Suspense

### *The Security Specialists*

*Deep Waters*

*Fatal Reunion*
*Protective Duty*
*Concealed Identity*
*Final Verdict*

# DEEP WATERS

## JESSICA R. PATCH

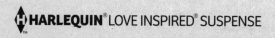

**HARLEQUIN**® LOVE INSPIRED® SUSPENSE

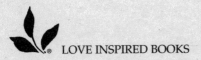

LOVE INSPIRED BOOKS

PLEASE RECYCLE
THIS PRODUCT IS RECYCLABLE

Recycling programs
for this product may
not exist in your area.

ISBN-13: 978-0-373-45721-2

Deep Waters

Copyright © 2017 by Jessica R. Patch

www.Harlequin.com

**Printed in U.S.A.**

When you go through deep waters and great trouble,
I will be with you. When you go through rivers of difficulty,
you will not drown...
*—Isaiah 43:2*

To Crimson:
Because I dedicated the *last* book to your mother,
and she passed down the love of sea turtles to you.
When you learn to read, thank her for this. Love, Auntie Jess.

Special Thanks to:

My agent, Rachel Kent; my editor, Shana Asaro;
my brainstorming partner, Susan Tuttle; and
Sara Turnquist for all your invaluable information on sea
turtles. Anything I've stretched for fiction's sake is on me.

# ONE

The full moon's radiance blanketed the ocean. Tides were high. The generous breeze swirled in from powerful waves, leaving nothing but briny air to fill Caley Flynn's nostrils as she tiptoed down the boardwalk to her favorite place in the whole world. Her fingers trailed the weathered wood railing as grains of sand collected under her newly manicured nails.

Seven hours from Atlanta, where she'd grown up, she'd made Turtle Bay, Florida, her home right out of vet school. A small and lovely tourist town nestled along the peninsula separating the Gulf of Mexico and Tampa Bay, it was known for an abundance of sea turtles—especially loggerheads that nested on the sandy shores—fine dining and glorious summers.

She slipped out of her hot-pink flip-flops with fading green palm trees and descended the sandy stairs onto the beach. She loved the way the powdery sand coated her feet. As she met the cool water, a sigh escaped her; she even relished the salty film the surf left in its wake. But mostly she loved this season. It was June and sea turtle nesting was in full swing. Through October she had the unique opportunity to study loggerheads, leatherbacks, green turtles and hawksbills as they swam to shore, burrowed a nest in the sand and deposited hundreds of eggs before swimming back into the depths of the sea. In the next couple of months, the hatchlings would make their trek to the water with nothing but the night's gentle light to guide them.

Caley had been on faculty as the head marine life veterinarian at the Arnold Simms Sea Turtle Rescue, Rehabilitation and Research Center since she'd moved here, thanks to a few strings pulled by her professor and mentor, Leo Fines.

Every day was overloaded, but at night…nights sometimes belonged only to her, and she enjoyed her solitary strolls. She'd had a lot on her mind lately trying to secure a new grant for the nonprofit center. The fund-raising gala was coming up, and she was in charge of making sure everything went off without a hitch. They needed this grant. They needed the donations from investors.

The foamy water teased her bare feet and ankles as wet sand slipped away with the undertow. She gazed up at the moon, gray clouds casting shadows across the dark water.

*Whoosh. Whoosh. Whoosh.*

The lull of the ocean reminded her that the world didn't have to be full of violence. All her life she'd lived with the fear that something bad could happen to her or a member of her family. She hailed from a long line of navy men and women who'd gone on to serve in some branch of law enforcement, purposely putting themselves in danger.

After her sister, Meghan, had died, she simply couldn't deal with it anymore and she'd journeyed as far away as she could. Away from her family and the danger that surrounded them daily.

Caley enjoyed her work. Enjoyed the people. Rescuing, rehabilitating and releasing sea turtles. Making them healthy. Educating the public. They had more volunteers this year than last. But the grant and donations rarely strayed from her mind.

Moving out into knee-deep water, she walked parallel with the shore. Seaweed, like mermaid's hair, fanned and raked across the water.

She even loved seaweed.

Wait.

Caley removed her glasses and used her worn-thin gray T-shirt to clear the spots of water, then looked again. Inching closer, her lungs turned to iron.

Dark hair. Not seaweed.

Her stomach convulsed, threatening to bring up her dinner.

Two more feet and the refreshing water chilled her bones, raising gooseflesh on her skin; a strangled scream erupted from her burning throat.

Mary Beth Whaling, a student here in the college intern program, floated listlessly in the tide. Eyes wide open. Skin translucent.

No. No.

She trembled as she checked for a pulse, knowing it would be absent. *How did this happen? When did this happen? Why?*

Fumbling for her cell phone in her back pocket, Caley glanced up and saw a kayak floating about ten yards out. She dialed 911. She and Mary Beth had just spoken at lunch. She'd mentioned going to bed early tonight and starting a new romance novel. One of the many things they had in common. Of all the female interns—of all twelve interns total—Mary Beth was her favorite. She reminded Caley so much of herself at nineteen. Just seven years ago.

Sirens wailed in the distance as she stayed on the line with dispatch.

The police and ambulance would be here any second.

What was Mary Beth doing out here alone? She never swam without a second person.

Unless she hadn't been by herself.

But why would someone leave her here without notifying authorities or the center if an accident had taken place?

Was it an accident?

A stream of questions bombarded her mind as she continued to stand by Mary Beth. Caley wouldn't leave her, wouldn't let the tide draw her out.

As blue-and-red lights flashed, a couple of faculty members still working at the center made their way to her along with other interns from the dormitory next door. Shock, tears, horror etched their faces, mirroring Caley's feelings.

Billy Reynolds, the young man Mary Beth had been dating, flew toward her, but the officers held him back.

"Mary Beth!" he hollered, voice cracking. "What happened? Caley, what's happened?"

Caley's chest constricted. She had no answers.

A large, bald man—by choice it appeared and not by age—squatted next to Caley. "Come on. Let the first responders do their jobs. I have questions."

So did Caley. She dropped Mary Beth's cold hand and let the officer on the scene lead her farther up the beach, away from the onlookers. "I'm Officer Wilborn."

"Caley Flynn. I work for the Arnold Simms Center. Just down that way."

He looked toward the center and nodded. "How did you know the girl?"

Caley rubbed her forearms. "She's part of the intern program. We take twelve each year. From all over the United States. She's from Oregon." Her parents needed to know. "I have to call her folks."

"We'll get to that. Do you know why she'd be out here this time of night and alone?"

Mary Beth was wearing her racing-back swimsuit. The one she kayaked in. "I can't believe that she was. Her younger brother died in their pool when no one was home and she promised her parents afterward she'd never go in the water alone." Why did she change her mind?

Officer Wilborn continued to pepper her with questions she had no answers to, then left her to ask questions among the interns.

Dr. Leonard Fines, her mentor and the director of the center, sidled up next to her, draping his lanky arm around her shoulders. "I overheard some talk. Looks like she drowned. The kayak belongs to the center. They pulled it in five minutes ago."

Caley leaned into her mentor. "I was responsible for these students. How am I going to face her parents?"

"I can make the call."

Caley shook her head. "No, I'll do it. Then I need to go through her things. I don't want her parents to have that burden, as well." Watching Mom and Dad go through Meghan's room had been devastating. "I can't believe she'd be out here at night on the water." The unsettling feeling wouldn't shake.

"Well, she was." Leo was only a few years older than Caley's father; of course he was less rigid than Dad. But then Dad had been navy. Her whole family was military and law enforcement.

"You sure you don't want me to call the Whalings?" Dr. Fines asked.

"No," Caley said, "I knew her best." Or she thought she did. She trudged up the beach and into her office right outside the research lab. After a prayer for wisdom, she called Mary Beth's parents. She knew exactly how they'd respond. The same way her parents had when they found out Meghan had died.

After she hung up with the Whalings, she cracked open a can of peach tea and forced some down her dry throat. She had no explanation for why Mary Beth had been out on the water alone. Neither had her parents. No way the medical examiner or law enforcement would give her any information, since she wasn't on the case or next of kin. But… She grabbed her cell phone and called her big brother.

Wilder answered on the second ring. "Caley? Everything okay? It's late there."

"I need a favor."

Rustling sounded over the line and a muffled thank-you. "Okay. What kind of favor? You sound upset. Are you hurt?"

*Heartbroken.* She relayed the events that had transpired. "I need someone to help me find out the truth."

"The truth sounds like she went out alone and a tragic accident occurred, kiddo. Let the police do their job."

Caley balled her fist. "Wilder, you always talk about your gut instinct and how it's usually right. Well, my gut says this wasn't an accident. Something isn't right. Can you just…just call and talk to someone?" Wilder knew people in law enforcement all over the world. He worked with them often in conjunction with his private security company, Covenant Crisis Management. "Please," she choked out.

The sound of a deep inhale traveled across the line. "I'm in Dubai. Escorting someone of importance to a conference or I'd come out there myself."

"I don't need you to come out. I want you to make a phone call. Get me some information. I'm going crazy." Caley scooted her peach tea aside, removed her glasses and pinched the bridge of her nose. "How often do I ask you for anything?"

"Counting Christmases?"

"Wilder, be serious," she huffed.

"Do you really think there's foul play?"

"I don't know but I have a sick feeling. Mary Beth was

a sweetheart. And if she was out there by herself, she had a solid reason." Caley owed it to Mary Beth and Mary Beth's parents to get to the truth.

"Okay. I know a homicide detective who works for the Turtle Bay police. Tom Kensington. Former marine. He's a good dude, and he owes me a favor. I'll call him and see what I can find out."

"Thank you, Wilder. I owe you."

"You can pay up by not nosing around on your own. If it's not an accident, then I don't want you in the line of fire. Understand?" Wilder's gruff command barked loud and clear.

"You know I won't." This wasn't her line of expertise. She steered clear of purposely risking her life, unlike Wilder and his team of soldiers. Caley hadn't inherited that gene. Or she'd buried it. Either way. "You'll call me as soon as you hear, right?"

"You know I will, kiddo." Wilder's voice softened. "I love you. Hang tight and…I'm very sorry."

That was the big brother she adored. Tough exterior, gooey middle. She missed him. "I kinda wish you were able to come out. I'm…scared."

A sigh filtered through the line. "I wish I could too, darlin', but I'm a phone call away, okay?"

"Okay," she whispered. "Love you." She hung up and closed her eyes. *God, why did this have to happen?* Caley didn't expect an answer. She never knew why these things happened. Never got an answer to why Meghan had to die the way she did. But her heart wouldn't let her stop praying, even if most of the time it felt one-sided.

She eyed her desk. Paperwork had mounted. She worked on some of it, her mind wandering. Giving up, she spent an hour organizing her office, but to no avail. Finally, she finished off her tea—Mama would pitch a fit if she knew she was drinking canned sweet tea—and headed for the aquarium. Open to the public on weekdays, this was one of her favorite places in the center. As she entered the room, the hum of the air-conditioning kicked on, the air filters in the tanks bubbled and a prickle ran up her spine.

Caley shivered.

The sense of being watched rippled across her neck. She turned to the windows. Nothing but the faint light from the small motel-turned-dormitory next door.

She backed her way to the main doors, turned to make sure they were locked, only to scream at the sight of a looming figure pressed against the tinted glass.

Shepherd Lightman ground his teeth and reined in his temper as he peered into the center's doors. He'd been in a heavy sleep—the first one in two months, thanks to one assignment after another. Twiddling his thumbs would typically be the death of him, but he'd been ready for this vacation. Flown into Tampa for some deep-sea fishing, then leaving for a sweet cruise to the West Indies in two days. *Vacation.* A word Wilder Flynn, his best bud and boss, didn't seem to understand.

*You're less than thirty minutes from her. You'll be back in bed before the sun is up, dude. Promise.*

Shep better be, and he *was* the closest to Caley Flynn. Twenty-nine minutes away to be exact. As if he hadn't thought about her being near enough to swing by and see for a minute. But he'd never have done it in a million years. Nope. He wasn't going near Turtle Girl unless he was instructed.

She was Wilder's baby sister for one. And for two, she was sweeter than Alabama tea and way out of his league. He might only have six years on her in age, but he had a lifetime in experiences he wished he'd never had. He couldn't help that. Couldn't help the way his gut tightened every time he saw her wide blue eyes. Her black-as-night hair on summer-bronzed skin.

But he'd been instructed. And here he was.

"It's me, Caley." Even now, skittish as a jackrabbit, she was a sight to behold. "Shepherd Lightman. I work with your brother at Covenant Crisis Management." He'd been with Wilder since he opened the agency. Been around Caley many times when she visited, but why would she remember a nobody like him?

Big round eyes narrowed and she unlocked the glass doors. "I know who you are, Shepherd. I just didn't expect you to be nose to the glass at my center." She let him inside. "*Why* are you here?"

"Orders." *Just check on her, Shep. Humor her. She's scared. She's never seen a corpse. Not anywhere but a casket. It won't be pretty. I'll make a few calls to Tom, get the real deal. Just sit with her until her mind is put at ease and she knows this was an accident. She's freaking clean out.*

"From your brother." He glanced around the aquarium. He'd never been here before. Huge photos of turtles lined the walls with information about each species underneath. Several tanks filled the room. Turtles inside each one. Smelled like fish to him.

Caley locked the doors and folded her arms, staring.

He stared back, panic creeping into his bones. Did she want…a hug or something? *Oooh nooo.* He wasn't the comforting type. He could take down a dude from about two thousand yards with a sniper's rifle, but "there theres" weren't his thing. "I'm really sorry about what happened tonight. You'll get through it."

Caley blinked, tilted her head.

"It's not easy seeing what you saw. Nightmares are normal."

Her pouty mouth dropped open.

"I'm not good at this." Heat flushed his neck and he shifted his weight. Yeah, he was closer distance-wise, but making people feel at ease wasn't his thing. Wilder should have sent Jody. She was a female. And Caley and Wilder's cousin. Had lots of words. Too many for his taste, but still. Shep was the worst at words. Worst at mushy-mush. He ground his jaw and sucked it up. "You need some physical contact?" *Say no.*

Caley's eyebrows shot north at lightning speed. "Physical contact?"

"You know a hug or pat or something?" He stood like a dummy, not even knowing what to do with his hands—hands skilled at war, inexperienced at comfort—so he jammed them in his cargo shorts' pockets.

"A hug? Or pat?" She crinkled her nose as if she'd gotten a whiff of a rotten odor.

"Or something," he muttered.

Caley slowly shook her head. "No. I don't need a hug or pat from you. I could use information, though. Like how did you get here so fast?"

"I was in Tampa."

"Wilder said he was making some calls. Did he change his mind and put boots on the ground? Are you going to the medical examiner's office for answers instead?"

Turtle Girl was an arsenal of questions.

She eyed his torso and neck. "You can stand down, soldier."

Shep hadn't realized he'd been tensed. But being around Caley Flynn made him nervous. He relaxed his shoulders. "He's still making calls to our contact at the police department and the medical examiner's office."

"So why did he send you?" she asked.

"To make sure you remain calm."

She snickered.

Why was that so funny?

"So offering some physical contact is your way of doing it?" A slender dark eyebrow rose.

Heat flushed his cheeks. "Well…no. Just seemed… I don't know, like, maybe you needed it, but it appears you're okay and don't." The woman sent his tongue into a knot. "Wilder said you were scared." And wished he was there. But he couldn't be. So he'd sent Shep. The last person she seemed to want here.

She slipped her bottom lip in her mouth. "I'm okay, Shepherd." She didn't seem 100 percent. "I was on my way next door to the dormitory to pack up Mary Beth's belongings."

"The vic?"

"The intern who died. *My* intern." She pursed her lips and headed for the doors, mumbling something about her brother being a dope.

"Sorry." He followed her, catching a hint of something fruity. She was like a ballerina, the kind that popped out of jewelry boxes. All slender and dainty. Her voice even sounded like a music box melody. He'd know. One of his many foster moms kept a box like that on her dresser. She also kept cash inside. Taking that cash had sent him straight back to the group home until another family thought they could love him into being a healthy boy, or until the government money for keeping him in their care wasn't worth it anymore. No one had wanted him.

"So that's why he didn't send Jody? You were thirty minutes away?"

He snorted. Nope, Caley Flynn didn't want him. "All you got is me, Little Flynn. Sorry to disappoint."

She frowned. "As you can see, I'm fine. If you want to get back to your work in Tampa, you can."

"It was a vacation."

"Oh. Well, now *I'm* sorry." She pushed open the door and waited for him to exit, then she locked it. "What are you doing there? Partying it up on the strip?" No contempt in her question. Neutral. But clearly his past preceded him.

"Nope." He hadn't lived that kind of lifestyle since he gave his life to Jesus in Afghanistan. But no one seemed to notice that. Just what he'd done beforehand.

"So what are you doing then?"

"Chartering a boat to deep-sea fish. Then boarding a cruise liner for the West Indies." He followed her across the parking lot into the sand. His shoes were going to be filled with it. "Was this a motel?" The soft pink stucco building was rectangular with palm trees flanking the double glass doors.

"Yep. The center purchased it several years ago and converted it."

"You live here?"

"Me? No. I live a few miles away. Little bungalow on the beach."

Shep stayed on her six into the cool building, condensation fogging the glass. "Live alone?"

She gave him a strange half smile, almost confused. "No. I live with my landlord, Miss Whittle. She's a sweetie."

Like Caley.

She turned left and strode down a long hallway. Soft hums of TVs and chatter carried from the rooms. Not that he expected kids to be asleep even after midnight, but he did expect more buzz after losing one of their own.

"Mary Beth's room is at the end of the hall." She pointed to the last door on the right. As they neared it, Caley slowed. "I can't believe she's gone," she murmured.

Against his better judgment, Shep rested a hand on Caley's shoulder and patted. "There there."

Caley let an exhausted chuckle loose and touched his hand. Hers was so small next to his. "Thanks, Shepherd." She seemed to mean it. Maybe he did all right. She unlocked the door, stepped inside and gasped.

* * *

Caley froze in Mary Beth's room. Nothing but a sliver of moonlight to outline the shadowy hooded figure by the window. He paused, then grabbed a brass lamp and chucked it toward her.

A force shoved her aside and she crumpled to her knees.

Shepherd used his forearm to knock the blow of the lamp away.

The intruder was already halfway through the window.

Lunging, Shepherd latched on to the attacker's leg, yanking him inside, but the assailant used his other leg and rammed it straight into Shep's nose, giving him enough leverage to scurry out the window.

Shep wiped the blood seeping from his nose. "You gonna make it, Little Flynn?"

"Yes. I'm fine." Dazed. Terrified. But alive.

"Good." Shepherd lurched out the window and disappeared.

Caley flipped on the dorm light, revealing the disaster before her. Drawers had been tossed. Papers and books littered the floor along with everything that had been on the top shelf of Mary Beth's closet. Even her mattress had been overturned.

She laid a hand on her heart, willing it to slow its pace.

What had the intruder been searching for? And why such a mess? Why not come in and meticulously comb through everything so no one would be the wiser? Especially if the break-in was related to Mary Beth's death, which was likely going to be ruled an accident.

But now?

Now, it was obvious foul play was at hand. This was too much to be a coincidence. So whoever had come in here like a tornado must have been desperate. The big question was what on earth did he want?

Caley rubbed her sore knee and sat on the edge of

the upturned mattress. Of all the people to send why did Wilder send Shepherd Lightman? If his imposing size wasn't enough to scare someone half to death, the menacing blue eyes, almost gray, and faint scar running through his right eyebrow separating the hairs was. He rarely spoke, but when he did his voice was unmistakable. Baritone. Full of grit and gravel and yet hypnotic. Nothing but rock-solid muscle. Had a record for longest shooting distance as a marine sniper. A point man for the Special Reaction Team. Shepherd Lightman was more machine than man.

Truth was, all Caley knew about Shepherd came from the stories Wilder and the others had told of him. Wild. Fast. A heartbreaker.

But something about his pitiful effort to comfort her actually did comfort her. Bless him. And now he was out there hunting down whoever tried to wallop her with a lamp, and no doubt when Shep did find him, a sheer look would have the intruder confessing everything.

Of all Wilder's team members, Shep was the only one who revved her heart rate up a notch. Wilder should have sent Beckett Marsh. He was like a brother to her. Or their cousin Jody. She was capable and way easier to talk to.

Shepherd poked his head in the window and Caley jumped.

"Sorry." He hopped back inside and surveyed the room. "He gave me the slip about a mile down."

"I guess my gut was right."

"You're a Flynn. I'd trust your gut." He poked around in the empty closet. "What's your theory?"

"How do you know I have a theory?"

"You're a Flynn." He ran his hand along the top of the closet shelf.

Caley pushed her glasses back onto the bridge of her nose and laid her theory on him.

"Well…" His voice sent a ripple through her belly. "I'm inclined to agree. This is desperation right here. And we interrupted him. So he may not have found what he was lookin' for." His voice only held a splash of Southern twang, though he was from Alabama. "What do you think he was after?"

"That I don't know." Caley kicked at loose clothing piled on the floor. "I don't want her parents to see this mess. But I know the police need to come in and take prints, even if that guy did have gloves on."

Shepherd studied her a moment, his gaze lingering on her face until she squirmed. "Let me call Wilder first. See if he can rush Tom at TBPD for answers on her death and if he can get someone out here to take prints. Then we can clean up the mess before her parents show up."

"Okay. What if they don't rule this death a homicide? What do we do?"

Shep's full lips twitched. "We do a little snooping of our own. I have my PI license in Florida. Most detectives have an overload of cases anyway. Your hunch and a tossed room isn't going to light a fire underneath them on an accidental death ruling."

She stepped closer to him, noticing a smear on his cheek and fresh blood dripping from his nose. She grabbed a tissue, careful not to touch the box, and held it up. "Shepherd, your nose is still bleeding."

He dabbed at it and pocketed the tissue while Caley paced the room. "Make the call. But I can't let her parents in here with the room like this. So tell him to find a way to get me an answer. And say please."

He nodded and made the call. Fifteen minutes later Wilder called back. Shep put him on speakerphone.

"They're ruling it accidental. I'm sorry, Caley. No defense wounds, abrasions. Nothing that indicates anything other than a terrible tragedy."

Caley's blood boiled and she felt some desperation of her own. "What about the dorm being ransacked? Someone threw a lamp at my head, Wilder!"

Silence for two beats. "I didn't know about a lamp." Accusation laced his voice and Shep rubbed his brow.

"Well, Shepherd blocked it but it was thrown at me nonetheless." She glanced at Shepherd, who was still frowning. "Did you even tell Tom about her dorm room?"

"I did. They can come out and take a report. That's about it. Anything stolen?"

"I don't know," Caley said, flailing her arms because she needed to do something. "Wilder, that girl was precious to me. I don't believe this break-in, tonight, after she's found dead, isn't connected. Do you?"

"It could be connected, but not necessarily because it's murder. Maybe someone knows her effects will be boxed up and given to her parents. Maybe she had something someone didn't want to be seen. Doesn't mean they killed her. Just means they wanted to get something before it was exposed. Might not even be anything criminal. You don't know enough to make the lines meet."

Unfortunately, Wilder had a point. "Fine. Thanks for helping me and sending Shepherd. I'm sure he'll be glad to get back to his deep-sea fishing." She smiled at Shep.

"Take me off speaker," Wilder demanded.

Caley rolled her eyes and Shep held the phone to his ear. A few grunts and short replies later, he hung up.

"Well?" Caley asked when he clearly had no plans to relay the private conversation.

Shepherd ran his hands across his short cropped hair, the color of wet sand. "He wanted my assessment of you."

Caley loved Wilder but he was ridiculous. "Oh really. And what, pray tell, is your assessment, Shepherd?"

"I said you were fine. Shaken up. But stronger than you look."

"I didn't hear any of that." All she heard was *yes*, *yep*, *yeah*, *no*. *Yeah*. *Okay*. But it still warmed her to know Shepherd thought she was stronger than she looked. Wait, did she look weak?

"He's ordered me to stick around until my ship departs, for added measure. So...you're stuck with me." He cocked his head and folded his arms across his massive chest, his muscles popping out from underneath his white T-shirt. "I'll need a place to bunk."

"I can get a hotel for you, or you can take an empty dorm room."

He dipped his chin. "We can look into things with more detail a little later."

Caley nodded as Shep studied the messy room, waiting on the police to come take a report and print the room.

So they'd start digging. What would they find? And at what cost would it come if they did discover what got Mary Beth killed?

# TWO

Caley jolted from the bare twin mattress as knuckles collided with the door outside the empty dorm room she'd stayed in after last night's events. Shoving a mass of hair from her face, she squinted at sunlight pouring through the window that overlooked the ocean.

"Caley? It's 0700. You crackin'?"

Crackin'? She was barely breathing. It had been nearly 4:00 a.m. before she had finally decided against driving home. After the police left and cleared them to clean up Mary Beth's dorm room, Caley met with Mary Beth's parents, who had rented a car after their flight landed. They'd grieved together and then she followed them to the Turtle Bay Police Department.

She hadn't mentioned the ransacking. She wanted more information before suggesting foul play to Mr. and Mrs. Whaling. They'd been exhausted and retired to a hotel a mile away. Back at the dormitory, Caley had made up a bed for Shep two doors down from hers, including fresh sheets, but she'd been too exhausted to throw any on her own tiny mattress. Her mouth felt like cotton and her eyes were swollen from crying herself to sleep.

"You alive?" he called. "I'm coming in if you don't answer."

"I'm fine," she rasped. *Could use some water.* "Give me

a minute already." Grabbing her glasses, she haphazardly shoved them onto her nose and yanked the door open to a freshly showered—and ridiculously good-smelling—Shepherd. He didn't particularly have a "look" but his jeans and black T-shirt could be branded the Shepherd Lightman style. "Not all of us can manage on four or less hours of sleep."

"Roger that." With his index finger, he righted her crooked glasses. Her blood heated. She was definitely awake now and no doubt looking a mess. Smoothing down her hair, she was suddenly more self-conscious of her disheveled appearance.

Shep leaned against the door frame. "I smell breakfast from the mess hall. You want me to rustle up your number one square for the day? Or I can stand outside the door."

"This isn't Buckingham Palace, Shep." Though, with that stoic face, he'd make a great solider standing guard at the gates. "I need ten minutes. I'll meet you at the *cafeteria*." A solider through and through. "I'm a fan of French toast." She shut the door and snatched the bag she normally kept in her office in case she worked into the late hours. She rarely wore makeup and it was easier to pull her long hair into a sloppy bun on her head or a ponytail. Today she went with down and wet. It'd dry quickly.

She opened the door fifteen minutes later.

Shep hadn't left.

"You did hear me say this wasn't Buckingham, right?" She slid by him and shook her head.

He fell into step with her. "Who is Billy Reynolds?"

She paused. "How do you know that name?"

"Social media. I did some research while you got some shut-eye. Quite a few photos of him and our vic—I mean… Mary Beth."

Caley ambled through the lobby and down the hall to

the cafeteria that had once been the motel's dining commons. "Did you sleep at all?"

"Who is Billy Reynolds? And what is his relationship with Mary Beth?"

Shep motioned for her to go ahead of him through the breakfast buffet line. The room was sparse today after last night's tragic events. Two interns sat at a table. They needed to call an assembly. In the back corner, Dr. Fines sat with a cup of coffee, stubble covering his chin and cheeks. He looked as haggard as Caley felt. "I need to go talk to Leo."

Eyebrows scrunching, Shep set his sights on her mentor and boss. "Leo? Leonard Fines?"

"Yes," Caley said, and left Shep in line with two trays. She hurried to Leo and he stood and hugged her.

"We need to rally the kids," he said.

"I know. I was just thinking that. But I have to tell you something first." She sat across from him and relayed the earlier events.

Leo pushed his coffee cup away. "You really think the two incidents are related?"

"I do. I don't have solid proof, but I mean, come on." She toyed with an empty creamer cup he'd used for his brew. "The police are ruling it an accident, but Shepherd is sticking around. In case it's not. At least for a couple of days."

Leo leaned forward. "Caley, if the police and medical examiner say it was an accident, then it was. I don't need to remind you that our biggest fund-raising gala is in a few short weeks, and if Nora Simms gets a whiff of scandal, your job and mine will be over. Not to mention we don't need donors pulling out."

Nora Simms was the daughter of Arnold Simms—one of the greatest marine biologists to ever live. His work with sea turtles was extraordinary and that's why the center was named after him. Nora had already threatened Dr. Fines's job and Caley's six months ago when protestors picketed outside the research lab. The media had skewed everything and a few donors pulled out, believing that their research was inhumane to turtles. As if. Nora had been furious. Ranting about her dad's life work going down the tubes.

But Mary Beth might not have accidentally drowned. Seeing her killer brought to justice was more important than their jobs.

"Leo, what if someone hurt Mary Beth? Do we tie a block to that possibility and let it sink to the ocean floor?"

Leo's face flushed. "Of course not, Caley. I'm not insensitive. But don't you think, if it had been a homicide, there would have been some evidence? Even a trace?" He clasped her hand. "The professionals ruled it out."

"But the dorm room was trashed. What about that?"

"Maybe someone heard she passed away and broke in to steal some of her belongings. Phone. Laptop. Cash. Who knows?" Leo had a point but the eerie feeling wouldn't shake loose.

Unsolved crimes happened all the time. "I'm going to look into it anyway, Leo. I have to. I'll be discreet." With Shepherd here and a contact at the police department, they could investigate, and if they turned up solid evidence, they'd cross that bridge when they came to it. "Two days." That's how long Shep would be around. Surely, by then he'd have a solid lead. "Nora won't have to know a thing. Our donors won't either."

Leo closed his eyes and heaved a sigh. "Fine, but be careful and keep the fact that her room was ransacked under wraps. No hint of a scandal. To anyone. This is my life's work. I won't lose my job over a hunch."

Caley swallowed and shoved the paper top into the empty creamer container. Thankfully, the interns had kept to their rooms while the police had done their job last night. "Okay." At the moment it was a hunch so that was fair enough. "I'll send a group text for the interns to meet us here in fifteen minutes. We need to talk about this. Supply some grief counseling if needed."

Leo nodded.

Caley found Shep with two trays at a table near the exit. Her tray was loaded with French toast and bacon. Who was he feeding? An army? She took her seat and sent out the text.

Shep held a strip of bacon in his hand. "What did your boss have to say?"

Caley groaned and delivered the conversation.

Shep only grunted and ate his bacon while studying the cafeteria. Interns trickled in. Some in tears, others unusually quiet. They'd been here since mid-May. Already, they were like family. Caley excused herself and tended to her team. When they'd all arrived, Leo spoke to them, offered counseling. Some of the interns wanted to hold a vigil and murmured plans.

Caley finally stood and said a few words about Mary Beth. When they dispersed, she caught up with Billy. That's when Shep made his way over to the beverage area. He poured a glass of juice while Caley talked. If he was trying to be invisible, that wasn't happening. Shep was larger than life.

"Billy, can you tell me anything? Why would she swim or kayak alone? Did she mention it?" Caley asked.

Billy leaned against the end of the table. Face pale. Eyes hollow. "She said she was going to bed early. Read a book or something. But she'd been distant the past week or two. I thought she was low-key dumping me." He shrugged. "I can't believe she'd go in the ocean alone. Makes no sense."

Caley put her arm around him. "I don't think she did. I

think something else is going on here, Billy. I have what I think is proof." The ransacking of her room had to be.

"What kind of proof?"

She promised Leo to keep the incident quiet. "I can't tell you that. We have to keep things on the down low for now."

Billy gaped but nodded. "You don't believe it was an accident, do you?"

"No. Anything out of the ordinary with her? Other than being distant?" Caley waited while he seemed to process the information.

"Ashley said she's sneaked out a few times but wasn't sure where she went. I figured she was cheating on me with someone else." Billy rubbed the back of his neck. "That wasn't like her. I can't think of anything else, Caley. I'm sorry."

Caley nodded and looked to Shep. Not a single reaction on his face. She turned back to Billy. "Thanks. I'll talk to Ashley."

She scanned the cafeteria for her. Ashley had come in with three other interns earlier. She must have gone back to her dorm room. Once they entered the hallway, Shep grunted.

"I'm not fluent in grunt. Sorry," Caley said.

"Do you have a curfew here?" he asked.

"No, they're adults. As long as they show up to work we don't pry into their private lives." Caley headed toward the hall of dorm rooms.

"Then why sneak? People only do that to hide something. Trashed room indicates someone looking for a hidden item of some kind. Drugs?"

Caley snorted. "Doubtful. Mary Beth was an outstanding student at the University of Oregon. She was looking forward to her career. This is a highly respected internship program and we vet our students thoroughly."

"Well, then the other reason for sneaking off at night is she met someone. It adds up. She breaks away from Billy. Hides it from her friends. Women like to talk about their men. If she's hiding him, then it's someone they wouldn't approve of or someone who needed it to remain a secret."

"You mean like a married man?" Caley froze in the hall. "No way."

Shep tossed a skeptical glance her way. "Not everyone holds the same moral compass in their hand as you do, Turtle Girl."

"Turtle Girl?"

Shep shrugged. "Fits."

Except it didn't. Neither did *Little Flynn* or Wilder's *kiddo*. Caley was a grown woman. Not an adolescent. Just because Shepherd and Wilder had six years on her didn't mean she was a child. She was a respected marine life vet. With her own home. Her own life. "Well, I don't like it," she said.

That garnered her another grunt.

"Back to Mary Beth." She switched subjects. "You think this mystery man—if there is one—killed her, then came back later and tossed her room, looking for some evidence proving they were in an illicit relationship?"

"It's a starting point. Nothing else to go on." He nudged her to get moving again. "Once we talk to this Ashley, maybe we'll know more."

Caley knocked on Ashley's door. A moment later, Ashley opened it and eyed Shepherd with a mix of confusion and what Caley could only define as intrigue. For a man as rough around the edges and intimidating as Shep, he held some physical qualities that would make a girl swoon.

Like his lips—heart-shaped top with a protruding lower one. Crazy-soft-looking. Paired with bluish-gray eyes framed by thick dark lashes, he had zero trouble attracting female attention. And that wasn't including the mysterious scar and superhero physique.

The rumors she'd heard said Shep had never been in a committed relationship, but he'd dated the way a man with a cold went through tissue. Box after box.

No, that wasn't the kind of man Caley was interested in. So the attraction had to stay simple. Appreciative. Besides, he was a soldier. And she'd vowed long ago that she wasn't marrying a soldier or a man who worked in law enforcement of any kind.

Too risky for the heart.

Shep narrowed his eyes. Uh-oh. He'd caught her gawking. She pushed her glasses up her nose. "This is my…" What was he? Her brother's friend? "Friend. He's stopped in for a visit."

Shep's eyebrow, the one without the scar splitting the hairs, rose.

"I wanted to talk to you about Mary Beth. Can I come in? We? Can we come in?" Caley asked and shoved her way inside, a good measure away from Shepherd.

"Sure," Ashley said, opening the door wider to accommodate Shepherd's frame to enter without brushing her. "I think I was the last person to see her. She was in the equipment room around eight last night."

Why would she be there? Unless she really was going out to kayak or fill the oxygen tanks for an upcoming dive.

"What's in the equipment room?" Shep asked.

"Boats, diving equipment, anything we use out on the water for work or play." Caley slumped on the edge of Ashley's bed. "Did she say if she was going out, Ashley?"

"No. She said she left her beach bag in there." Ashley pawed her face. "If I'd pressed for the truth maybe this wouldn't have happened. I knew she was lying and I let her. To each her own, you know?"

"Sure. How did you know she was lying?" Caley asked.

"She'd been going out late at night. Several times in the past few weeks. I approached her about it, but she said she wanted to be alone. Not to worry. But why would you want to be alone that late at night? She seemed shifty. Distant."

"That's what Billy said," Caley said.

"I think she was cheating on him. Or about to break it off for good." Ashley collapsed in her desk chair. "Billy thought so too."

Shep might be right. There could be a mystery man involved. "She never confided in you? About another guy?"

"No. She knows how tight me and Billy are. I guess she thought I'd tell him. But I wouldn't have."

"Anyone else she might have talked to?"

"Toby. He never liked Billy much. And Mary Beth had been spending a lot of time down in the lab with him. At first I thought maybe they had something going on, but he's engaged and a stand-up guy. I don't see him cheating. And honestly, I don't see Mary Beth doing something like that either."

Neither did Caley. Shep's eyes held skepticism.

"If you remember anything else, please tell me."

"I heard her parents came last night and took her stuff. A few of us went to her room this morning and it was empty. Like she was never even here." A tear leaked from her eye. "I can't believe this."

Caley wrapped her in a hug. "I know. If you need anything, call me." They left her room and were down the hall when Shep spoke.

"Let's check out the equipment room. See if we can find that bag she was hunting for. If there was a bag. Maybe there was something of extreme importance in it. Something that got her killed."

"Okay. And I hate to think it, but you might be right, Shep. She might have met someone who needed to stay a secret." And if that were the case, they had to find him.

\* \* \*

Shep had rolled the interviews with the interns around in his head in between trying to figure out why Caley had been gawking at him outside Ashley's door earlier this morning. Like she was admiring him in a more than friendly way.

He'd shoved the ridiculous notion aside and followed Caley around for the remainder of the morning, keeping out of her way while she worked. He and Caley had lunch once again in the cafeteria, and now they were inside the aquatic center, where he stood in the hub of a group of tourists while Caley shared sea turtle migration patterns and habits and advances in research.

The passion in her voice held his attention captive along with the thirty other tourists hanging on every word. But he had to pull his thoughts away from her hypnotic voice and focus on the case and his plans to keep Caley protected if the intruder from last night returned. A possible murder wouldn't stop Caley from her daily routine. Life had to go on. Just like in war. No way to make time freeze when a comrade had been lost. Fighting and protecting lives didn't come to a standstill because people grieved. Caley wasn't a solider like most of the Flynn family, but she was proving she was a fighter by standing here continuing with her spiel on sea turtles and not crawling into a hole to hide.

He admired that about her. Admired her brain. The woman was ridiculous smart. And gentle. Patient. Okay, this was not pulling his thoughts away. This was fixating on a woman who was so out of his league it wasn't even funny. Back to the assignment.

The best working theory was Mystery Man wanted to stay hidden, which explained his motive to toss Mary Beth's room, looking for a piece of evidence that would have exposed their relationship. But why kill her? Had she threatened to tell someone about them? Tracking down Mary Beth's actions over the past few days was imperative, but no one seemed to know where she'd been.

Someone was lying.

Twelve interns working and living together day after day and no one could tell them where the girl went? Shep wasn't buying that.

Caley finished her talk and handed the crowd off to another staff member and photographer. Tourists loved their pictures.

Caley shoved her glasses on the bridge of her nose—he could tighten those for her if she wanted—and strolled toward him. "Did I bore you?"

"No." *Boring* would be the last adjective to describe Caley Flynn.

"You even listen?"

Had she wanted him to? "I know loggerheads can get up to three hundred pounds and fishing gear is their biggest threat because they can get caught in longlines." He enjoyed the satisfaction of seeing mild shock on her face. Yeah. He listened. Hard not to.

But then she grinned and it sent a blip to his heartbeat. "Have you ever seen them swimming in their habitat? It's amazing."

"Maybe," he said. "To be honest I wouldn't know one turtle from the next, but I planned to do some diving off the cays. On my cruise. Now, I'll know that the leatherback's carapace is black with white splotches while the green turtle has a light or dark brown carapace. And it's sometimes shaded with olive. Oh, and the carapace is the hard upper shell."

Caley pulled her glasses off and studied him. Had he passed the test? Her narrowed eyes said she might be about to fail him. "Are you certified to dive, soldier?"

"Yes," he said warily.

"Like navy good or just marines good?" A hint of teasing flickered in her eyes. Caley Flynn may not be military but the navy coursed through her veins by birth.

"Good enough not to need a babysitter."

She glanced around. "I'll tell you what. Since you've been such a trooper today, and I need to run out to one of the dive sites anyway, I'll let my team and interns know I'm leaving and we'll check some longlines, make sure no turtles are caught. Then we'll do a little diving before coming back to shore. It's a place Mary Beth and I dived—a favorite spot of hers. Maybe someone who runs the excursions might know something or has seen her diving with someone other than me or an intern."

Shep saluted. "Okay."

After one last tour at the aquatic center, Caley rustled Shep up a scuba suit, gear and tank. She drove to the marina and led him to the center's boat. "All aboard," she teased.

Shep dropped his scuba gear next to Caley's and shook his head. Not only was her tank hot pink but her flippers and scuba suit had an equally pink stripe running down them. The ultimate girlie-girl.

"I see you pooh-poohing my gear, solider. It's not a crime to love to pink."

She cranked the engine and brought the boat to life, then guided them from the mainland out to sea. He'd give her a pass on the pink gear since she handled the boat like a boss. Wind on his face, sun warming his back, Shep was once again impressed. The taste of salt coated his lips and he licked them as they continued farther out, the sandy beaches becoming nonexistent.

He picked up the tank again, inspected it. Severe pink. "It should be a crime," he insisted.

She raised her sunglasses on her head and studied him. "Are you joking? I can't tell."

He hollered over the buzz of the motor. "Yes, I'm joking."

She slowed the boat down and they floated toward a huge longline—Shep had fished this way a few times. Attached to the line were baited hooks. Probably after halibut or swordfish. Bright orange buoys marked the spots.

"Fisherman will probably be back in the morning." She suited up below deck, then came back up. Looking perfect in pink. "Just gonna take a quick look. Make sure no turtles are caught on the hooks. I'll be up in five, ten minutes."

He almost balked at her diving alone, but she was an expert and he trusted her.

She sat on the edge of the boat, and fell backward, gracefully, into the water. Shep watched until her hot-pink tank disappeared. In about six minutes, she surfaced. "No turtles. Let's ride out to Soldier's Reef."

Back in the boat, she zipped across the water, smooth as glass, and toward the artificial reef. "We're two hundred yards from shore. Only going down about forty feet, but, man, just you wait. It's awesome." Her eyes lit up and she didn't waste any time as she increased the throttle until they arrived to their diving destination. "Gonna moor the boat and we're good."

She took a line and tied it to the cleat of the deck, then passed the other end through the eyebolt of the pickup line on the buoy before securing it to the second cleat. Something about the professionalism and quick way she worked...she wasn't just a girl with her nose inside a turtle shell all day. There was even more to Caley Flynn than Shep had realized, and he happened to like it all. Way too much.

"I guess we'll chat with the charter boats that bring tourists out after we dive?" he asked.

"That's the plan," she said as she grabbed her mask. "They're all out on tours anyway."

"Hey, where are your glasses?" He hadn't seen her without them once.

"Contacts. I hate wearing them but I haven't gotten around to getting a prescription diving mask." She shrugged. "Well, let's get this party started. Not to sound like a brochure but you're about to see a spectacular site. This whole reef was built from waste. Like pipes, army tanks and even a navy WWII aircraft carrier."

"Sounds interesting."

She nodded enthusiastically. "It was created as a memorial to those who serve our country." Her voice softened as she sat on the edge of the boat, back facing the water. "Like you."

"Then I'm ready to see it, Little Flynn." If he continued to call her that, he might remember how completely off-limits she was. Shep pulled his mask over his face, inserting his mouthpiece. Over the boat he fell, then flipped onto his stomach and a whole new world opened up. Sunlight filtered into the underwater paradise. Murky but gorgeous. Masses of spiky coral jutted north from the reef. Thousands of tiny silver fish maneuvered in the water.

Caley held up the *okay* sign with her hand and he signaled back. She pointed and swam like a regal dolphin as he trailed. A spotted eagle ray scurried from the sandy surface, stirring up the ocean floor. Caley skimmed the creature with her fingers.

He marveled at the array of colors. Like a living rainbow underneath here. Banana yellow, ruby red, neon blue, orange. One sight after another.

But the brightest, most enticing sight was in black and hot pink.

And it was the one creature down here, or above, he wanted to study most but couldn't. Caley Flynn was everything he admired and that astonished him. He wished he could protect her from all that she'd seen in the last twenty-four hours, help her keep her innocence in a dark world.

A burst of emotion he'd never experienced—couldn't even put a name to—flooded his chest, and he resolved right here, right now that he'd do everything in his power, work tirelessly, to find out what happened to Mary Beth Whaling. A need greater than he'd ever experienced burrowed into his marrow. A need to come through for this woman.

No matter the cost.

# THREE

Caley never tired of marine life. Silence except for the gentle sounds of air bubbles releasing. She reached down and felt the hose releasing oxygen from her tank to her mouthpiece. Still had sufficient tension. She kept an eye on Shep, studying him. Powerful legs. Powerful in general. Understanding dawned as to why Wilder had brought Shep into his team. He was a force to be reckoned with. A true soldier in every way. Caley admired the men and women in the military. Loved this reef dedicated to their honor. Seemed Shep did too.

He was admiring a barracuda with sharp teeth, nearly five feet long. Fierce. Seemed the fish and the solider studying him had something in common. She left him to his amusement as a goliath grouper swam around a crag revealing a green turtle nested in the crevice. She swam toward it, breaking up a school of bluish-green pompano, then reached the gentle creature, brushing her hand along its smooth carapace.

*Carapace.* Shepherd had been listening. Watching the tour. But it seemed as if he'd been preoccupied with something else too. Probably the case. But when he'd been able to relay what she'd said, it had sent a thrill through her. Her own family, while supportive, never listened with such attentiveness to her passion for marine life—for sea turtles.

She stroked the turtle again; it was probably hunting for root algae. *Eat on, big guy. Eat on.*

She breathed in. *Huh.* Short breath. Strange. She squeezed the hose again. Sufficient tension. She should have been given a full breath.

An odd sensation crept up her back.

She grabbed her pressure gauge. Twenty-thousand PSI. Plenty of pounds of pressure. So why the limited flow of oxygen?

She breathed in again, watching the gauge.

Another short breath. But even more frightening was the way the pressure dropped dramatically. How on earth?

Her heart lurched into her throat as she inhaled again. Nothing.

Her air supply was completely cut off! No warning.

*Stay calm. Don't panic.*

Shep was about five feet away. They could share air.

Turning, Caley saw only the underwater world.

No Shep.

She fumbled for her tank rattler to signal him. Surely he'd hear it…but it wasn't hooked on her belt like it normally was.

Her brain screamed for air.

Swiping her knife, she clanged it against her oxygen tank.

*God, please let him hear me! I pray* You *hear me!*

Turning upward she had two choices and not much time to decide which option was best. Caley could hope Shep had heard her banging and that she could hold out until he arrived with oxygen, or she could make an emergency ascent.

Up thirty feet.

Exhaling the entire time so her lungs didn't expand and do catastrophic damage.

Could she exhale that long?

Every fiber in her being convulsed.

What to do?

Time was running out.

She needed to breathe!

Shep was nowhere.

No time.

She bolted for the surface.

Heart beating out of her chest.

Up she raced, slowly exhaling…exhaling…exhaling… Not too fast. *Can't stop exhaling.*

She desperately needed air.

Anxiety continued to rise but she'd been trained. *Don't panic. Keep exhaling.*

*God, help me!*

Something tugged at her leg.

She kicked, then realized it was Shep. She used her hand and made a slicing signal across her throat as she continued to exhale and rise.

Maybe fifteen feet left.

He grabbed her forearm, pulled her closer to his chest, removed his breathing apparatus and handed it off to her.

Caley wrapped her hands around his as he held it to her, inhaling sweet oxygen, then she passed it back to him as they made their ascent more slowly to the surface, their knees sometimes knocking together as they kicked upward.

He signaled the *okay* sign and she gave it back. Relief flooded her, but also the unsettling vibe over what had occurred.

They made their way to ten feet where they had to wait the three excruciating minutes for a decompression. Shep grabbed her pressure gauge and hose and studied it while they passed off air to one another, waiting.

She'd been on hundreds of dives. Could teach a class if necessary. This had never happened before.

With Mary Beth's death on the edge of her mind, several frightening scenarios popped through her brain. And questions.

Shep dropped her gauge. His eyes narrowed. Two more minutes and they could talk this out. But for now it was just them.

The ocean that had once been peaceful and calm now took on an ominous appearance as if it was disappointed it hadn't swallowed her up whole.

She shivered and concentrated on breathing. On Shepherd.

Sharing the apparatus with him felt intimate even though it was nothing more than a means to stay alive. Wanting to spring to the surface, to safety, she checked her watch.

Time was up.

She nodded and they finished their ascent, bursting into the atmosphere, inhaling all the oxygen they needed. Warm sunshine. Seagulls squawking.

"What happened?" Shep growled, all grit and gravel in his voice.

"I don't know," she said as she hauled herself into the boat, Shep right beside her. She removed her tank and studied it. "I just don't know. One minute I had air, then a short breath, then nothing. I filled it up two days ago and haven't been out since then."

Shep studied the tank. "Didn't Ashley say Mary Beth was in the equipment room the night before she died?"

Shep's unspoken accusation was absurd. "Mary Beth did not tamper with my tank. Besides, she wouldn't be skilled enough to know how. I don't even know what happened."

"But it's possible."

"It's insane. What would her motivation be?"

"I don't know." Shep tossed his mask on the bench and frowned out at the sea. "We need to get a scuba tech to check it out. And not one from the center."

Caley shook out her wet hair. "Why?"

"I don't trust anyone there." He faced her. "I don't think this was an accident. Just like Mary Beth's death wasn't. And if I'm right, someone on the inside wanted you to run out of air. Could have been Mary Beth."

Caley's legs felt like jelly and she collapsed on the bench. "That makes no sense. I always dive with a partner. Whoever did it would know I'd have a buddy to breathe with."

"Maybe whoever did it had planned to go with you. Maybe Mary Beth. What if she conveniently disappeared and you didn't make your ascent safely? What if she lured you farther down?"

Caley's stomach curdled. "I can't…believe that." Why would anyone want to harm her? Or Mary Beth? "If it was Mary Beth who messed with my gear, why did she end up dead? You think someone knows and killed her for it?"

"I don't know why. But this whole scenario isn't jibing."

"I don't always keep my gear in the equipment room. Most of the time I keep it on the boat. Anyone could have access. It could have been tampered with long before I brought it to the equipment room."

"Either way, someone knows you use a hot-pink oxygen tank."

Caley's throat burned. "It could have been an accident."

"Maybe." Shep sat beside her. "But maybe not, Little Flynn. Maybe not."

Shaken to the core, she hoped Shep would reach out with another weak "there there," but he didn't.

"I'm gonna call Wilder. Update him."

Like a good soldier.

"Let's get to shore and talk to personnel, see if Mary Beth dived with anyone not connected to the center. Then we can take the tank to the university and have it checked out by a random tech. If it's not an accident, then call Wilder. Let's not worry him until it's necessary."

Shep sniffed, seemed to mull the idea over. "All right."

What if Shep's guess was right? What if someone had planned to go diving with Caley and *had* thought to lure her farther below and disappeared? Which prompted her next question. "Where were you? One minute you were checking out a barracuda and the next, I couldn't find you." She wasn't accusing him but she was curious. Five feet apart was too far to begin with, but out of eye sight was unacceptable, though easy to do, especially if you weren't a regular diver.

He ran his hand through his hair. "I shouldn't have gotten too far away. I failed you, Caley."

Was he joking? "Shepherd, I'm not sure I could have made it all the way up. And there is no decompressing on an emergency ascent. I'm not fussing at you." She laid her hand on his. "I just wondered."

He snatched his hand away and stood. "Let's get moving."

She cranked the engine. So much for accepting some grace. Maybe he'd accept this next gesture. "I meant to say something earlier—those twin beds are tiny at the dorm. I'm going to get you a hotel room. Do you want to be closer to the center or to my house? I live on the other side of town on a small residential strip of beach property. But there's a quaint little B and B nearby." Not that Shepherd looked like B and B material.

"How long will it take a tech to discover if the tank was tampered with?"

Okay, not accepting that extension of grace either. She sighed. "Depends."

"Then I'll make a decision later."

Ah. That made sense. If it was a direct threat to Caley, he'd want to be close in order to protect her. If it wasn't, he might opt for a hotel farther away. That sort of stuck in her craw. But then why would he want to be near her for any other reason than to follow Wilder's orders? Why did it matter?

Caley increased the throttle and headed back to the marina to dock, then they headed to the dive tour facility. According to them, Mary Beth hadn't been diving with anyone other than interns and Caley. They zipped to the university and dropped off the tank with a reputable researcher in the marine biology department.

"I used my extra bag last night, so do you mind if we stop by my house so I can change?" Caley noticed how cramped Shep's legs were in her yellow Volkswagen Beetle. She couldn't help that.

"Sure. So you rent a house and your landlord lives with you? That's weird." He took off his mirrored aviator glasses, using his shirt to clean the smudges.

"Well, I rented the whole bungalow until a year ago when Miss Whittle had some health problems and couldn't live alone anymore. Her only son lives in Montana. She won't do the cold. He owns a ranch and wouldn't move here—real nice guy, huh? Anyway, I offered her a room. I mean, it is technically her house. I can look after her and… I don't know… I like it. Plus she cut my rent by more than half. She reminds me of my grandmother."

Shep wouldn't know the love and warmth of a grandmother. He'd never had one growing up in foster care. Her heart ached for the little boy Shepherd once was. No family. No real home. No grandparents to bake for him or dote on him.

"Do you have a single mean bone in your body, Little Flynn?"

*Little Flynn.* She had to get him to stop using that term. It was annoying. "I don't care for that term just so you know."

"Nothing wrong with being a Flynn." His voice almost sounded covetous. Guess she couldn't blame him. The Flynns were tight-knit. Demanding and rigid at times, sure, but they loved one another and displayed affection to show it. Dad's hugs were almost as suffocating as Wilder's. But she treasured them nonetheless.

"It's not the *Flynn* I don't like. It's the *Little*."

Shep sized her up. "You are little."

"I'm not a baby."

"You're Wilder's baby sister."

She heaved an exasperated sigh. "I'm his younger sister. Difference." She turned right at the traffic light past several tourist shops selling knickknacks, souvenirs, surfing equipment and, of course, T-shirts with Turtle Bay stamped on them.

Shep didn't respond to her last retort, so she let it go. Besides, they were home. She pulled into the driveway and under the carport to her three-bedroom, two bath, bungalow-style home. It sported banana-yellow stucco with a bright red chimney and a welcoming white door. Palm trees surrounded the home and one stood guard at the yellow concrete stairs leading to her cozy porch.

"Welcome to my house. It's not much but it's home." She put her key in the lock but the door opened. "Well, that's odd," she mumbled.

"What?"

"We don't leave the doors unlocked. I mean, it's safe here in Turtle Bay but…"

Shep guided her back a step. "I'll go in first," he whispered.

"Sure…okay." Chest pounding, Caley balled her fist and rubbed it against her thigh. "Wait! Let me go. Miss Whittle may have checked the mail and forgotten. With her heart condition, your barreling in could send her into cardiac arrest."

Shep didn't look like he was going to let her but then he scooted over. "Just holler. Don't go in."

"She's almost deaf. If she's not wearing her hearing aids, she wouldn't hear a train if it roared past her window."

Heat flashed in Shep's eyes. "Pray her heart holds up then, because you're not going in there before me."

She tamped down on her temper. "Fine, but holler first."

Shep entered. "Miss Whittle!" Scuffling sounded from inside and something crashed on the tile floor. "Miss Whittle!"

Shep sprinted through the living room and into the kitchen. Caley followed and tripped over a throw pillow from the rocking chair. The house was a wreck! It mirrored Mary Beth's dorm room. Couch cushions, books and magazines had been scattered across the living room floor. "Miss Whittle!"

Caley rushed into the kitchen. Through the window by the breakfast nook, she spotted a man dressed in dark clothes and a hoodie darting across the backyard toward the road. Shep was hot on his heels.

"Miss Whittle?" *Lord, please let her be safe.* Where could she be? Panic welled up in her chest.

She rounded the eating bar and gasped, covering her mouth with her hand. Miss Whittle lay on the floor, blood trickling down her brow and cheek. Caley grabbed her cell phone. Déjà vu. Feeling for a pulse, she called dispatch for an ambulance and police.

There it was. Faint.

"Yes, she has a pulse, but she also has a heart condition," she informed the dispatcher. Caley held Miss Whittle's hand and prayed God would keep her heart working and that everything would turn out all right...even though, deep down, Caley wasn't so sure she believed her prayers made a difference. They hadn't protected Meghan, and Caley had prayed daily for the protection and safety of her family.

She continued to hold Miss Whittle's hand as she fretted for Shep. Where was he? Had he caught the guy this time? Was it the same guy who broke into Mary Beth's dorm room?

And why would he break into Caley's place? She didn't have anything that belonged to Mary Beth.

Once again sirens blared and first responders rushed to the house, where they took Miss Whittle's vitals. The police arrived, but this time Officer Wilborn wasn't on the scene. Instead, a man dressed casually caught her attention. Tall. Muscular. Caley had seen enough plainclothes officers to know this was one.

"Miss Flynn," the man said, "I'm Detective Tom Kensington. A friend of your brother's."

Wilder and Shep's contact at Turtle Bay Police Department. "Yes, of course. Thank you for coming." First responders left with Miss Whittle to take her to Turtle Bay Hospital. As soon as Caley finished here, she'd call Miss Whittle's son, then go to the hospital to be with her.

"Can you tell me what happened?" he asked.

They came home.

Shep chased the intruder.

No, she didn't get a good look at him except to notice he was wearing a black hoodie. In this weather.

"I'm going to be honest with you, Caley. It's suspicious. Two break-ins. One deceased girl. But there are no real dots to connect. I need more substantial evidence. But since you're a Flynn and I owe Wilder a solid, I'm going to do what I can, off the books, because Turtle Bay tax dollars won't let this dog hunt. Her death was ruled an accident and it appears to be so. As far as this isolated incident, they'll process everything. When I hear something, I'll let you know."

She clutched her chest. "Thank you. Off the books is fine." Especially after what Leo said about a potential scandal.

The kitchen door swung open and Shep trudged inside. He shook his head. "He jumped in a van about three blocks up the beach. I didn't have time to get the plates." He spotted Detective Kensington and grinned. "Tom."

"Shepherd. Good to see you again." They shook hands, and Detective Kensington told Shep the same thing he'd told her. "You get much of a look at that van?" Tom asked.

"White van. Commercial. Guy was medium height. Hundred seventy pounds." Shep rubbed the back of his neck. "I appreciate you looking into this quietly. Caley's boss isn't thrilled about what's happening given the gala they have coming up. Scandal is a bad thing. So quieter is better until we can pinpoint what's going on."

Caley's stomach dipped. Again, Shepherd had been paying attention to her needs and he was protecting not only her but her career. She wasn't sure what to do with that.

"I understand. I'll keep you posted. You do the same." Tom shook Shepherd's hand again. "You keeping busy since last time I saw you?"

"Fair amount."

Tom chuckled and looked at Caley, jerking a thumb

in Shepherd's direction. "This guy right here? One of the craziest guys I ever met. Hard core. No fear."

Caley swallowed hard. "I believe it," she rasped. The exact kind of man she would never attach herself to. "I tend to like a quieter life."

"Sorry things have shaken up for you," Tom said. He glanced at Shepherd, whose neck had flushed. Was he angry at Tom's words? "But this guy will keep you safe and I'll do what I can on my end."

Tom left with his report and Caley stared at Shepherd.

"I'm not reckless." Shepherd's voice came with a gravelly hard edge.

"I didn't think you were, or that Tom implied that. I think he admires and respects you as a brave soldier." She was thankful he was fearless. But while he wasn't reckless, crazy meant going into dangerous missions with no fear of dying. No worries. No concerns. He had been point man for the Special Reaction Team in the Marine Corps. Yeah, she was familiar.

That's why Wilder hired him right off the bat and bragged about Shep. He had experience in crisis situations. Terrorist attacks. Hostage situations. VIP protection. Out of the nine-member elite team, Shep was positioned at the front. Leading the entry element.

No fear of death. Of leaving a loved one behind. That nagged her. And it shouldn't.

His jaw flexed. That had seriously rubbed him wrong. "How's Miss Whittle?"

"I don't know. I need to get to the hospital." Her body felt like a waterlogged tree trunk, exhaustion seeping into every pore. What was happening to her perfect little world? Why was it crumbling like wet sand? Sunshine had turned to storm clouds. Torrential rains had fallen.

And she was falling apart.

"I'll drive you over there. Go get cleaned up and—" he

surveyed the disaster "—and I'll start putting this back together."

Right now what she needed wasn't a fresh change of clothes. Or a clean house.

Right now, she needed…comfort. A hug from Dad or Wilder.

All she had was Shep.

He'd quickly proven he was able to protect her physically. But she needed emotional security and that wasn't his strong suit.

"You hear me? You'll feel better if you clean up."

No. She wouldn't. He was all she had right now. She inched toward him, his eyes narrowing further with each step. When she reached his personal space, he backed up.

*Don't run from me, soldier.* She needed solace and safety from strong, able arms.

He backed up until the kitchen counter blocked his getaway.

She slipped her arms around Shep's waist and rested her head on his chest, listening as his heart rate kicked up. Waiting for him to reciprocate.

A hug.

What she desperately needed.

His body went rigid.

"I know this isn't part of your assignment, but I need physical contact, Shepherd. A hug. A pat. Whatever."

Slowly, his arms encircled her. Awkward, but there. The warmth of his hands seeping through her T-shirt.

"And don't say 'there there'—just tell me everything is going to be fine." She buried her face into his T-shirt, the smell of soap and total ruggedness rushing her senses. She inhaled and exhaled as his arms held her close.

"Everything's gonna be fine." His voice faltered but held enough confidence that she believed him. She pressed into his broad chest, like an iron wall that no one could penetrate. A force to be reckoned with. Here, sheltered by him, no one could touch her. And that brought more comfort than she was expecting. Dad and Wilder could make her feel safe and protected, but this…this was different. Terrifying. Exhilarating.

She clung to him.

He didn't push her away. Didn't tighten his grip on her either.

But he had her. He wasn't letting go and that meant something. At some point, though, he would let go. He'd leave her. For a cruise. And that sent a ripple of fear down her spine. Someone was hunting for something she didn't have. Someone who would keep coming. "Why would anyone think I have a single thing worth taking?"

"You were close to Mary Beth. She confided in you."

True.

"And if he didn't find what he was after that night in her dorm room, he may think you did." His breath ruffled her hair.

"But Miss Whittle." A hiccup escaped her lips and she pushed down tears as she fisted his shirt.

"I know." His hands pressed in on her back, but didn't move. Didn't caress or offer any added solace. He wasn't a comforter. He was a soldier.

Time to let him abort the mission. She broke the contact.

His eyebrows furrowed and he pursed his lips before shoving his hands in his pockets.

Caley put some distance between them. "We should go to the hospital. I can clean up later."

"Roger that, Little Flynn." He cleared his throat and clomped to the front door. Had she crossed a line? Was hugging her that unbearable?

"Shepherd, you're doing all you can. You don't feel

guilty do you?" He'd noted that he'd failed her before. But he hadn't.

"I'm fine. It's 1815 hours. You need to eat. I'll get you something at the hospital cafeteria." He opened the door, waiting for her.

She glanced around the room one last time. How was she ever going to solve this nightmare when she didn't have a single lead? And what would happen if the oxygen cylinder had been tampered with and each incident was linked? Nora Simms wouldn't see tragedy. She'd see news media and scandal. She'd see donors pulling out and dollar signs slipping away along with her father's legacy and life achievements. And Caley and Leo Fines would be out of a job they both adored. But she couldn't put her career above the life of Mary Beth.

So why would anyone else?

Last night had been painfully long for Shep. It was easier for him to get in, accomplish the mission and move on to the next one. That's how he'd been living his life since he'd joined the marines at eighteen. No need for feelings. Shut them off. Be a soldier.

But he never truly shut them off. Only shoved them down. All the resentment, anger, hurt from his childhood. The terror from war. The death tolls. The loss. Buried deep.

Until he'd given his life to Christ.

A weight had lifted, but even then Shep had made sure to keep the most painful things locked away. They were too hard to deal with and he wasn't going to curl up in the fetal position and cry like a baby.

But when Caley wrapped her arms around him, burrowing against him…something had cracked loose. He couldn't put his finger on it, but he rubbed his chest hoping it would soothe the ache that thumped there.

It had throbbed all night as he sat in a waiting room chair while Caley had kept vigil at Miss Whittle's bedside.

Didn't look like Miss Whittle's son needed to fly in, though he had offered. She had been cleared to come home this morning at 0900.

Now, Shep sat in one of Caley's Adirondack chairs, holding the phone to his ear and waiting for his Alpha Charlie from Wilder. But he'd take his reprimand like a good soldier. He'd let some dude give him the slip. Twice. Meaning Caley was still a sitting duck.

Shep had been trained to take down an enemy. Didn't matter if he wasn't familiar with the landscape. He should have taken the guy to the ground, gotten answers and been on the cruise liner to the West Indies—the next mission. No feelings involved. Wilder answered and Shep gave him the rundown of events.

"So you have no leads? Nothing to give Tom?" Wilder asked. His voice remained calm. Too calm. Shep knew Wilder well enough to know it meant a storm was brewing underneath his tone.

Bearer of more bad news. "No. We have a theory."

"Oh! A theory. Well, of course. That'll solve this case." Sarcasm. Wilder's typical way to reply when he was frustrated. *Welcome to the club, bro.* "A theory is nothing more than a good guess. You aren't going to find squat on a good guess."

"You don't say?" Shepherd bit the inside of his cheek. Wilder was his boss and his friend, but he didn't need a further verbal bashing. He was beating himself up nice enough.

"And if this person thinks my baby sister has something— something that might hurt him—then he's not through with her yet, Lightman."

"You're not telling me anything I don't already know,

Flynn. If you don't think I'm capable, take me off the assignment."

Wilder sighed. "It's my sister. The only sister I have left, Shepherd. And I'm stuck clear across the world. I'm on edge."

*Apology accepted.* But it nagged Shepherd that Wilder would have relieved him had he been in the country.

"You think the professor is shady?" Wilder asked, the brewing storm settling.

"Definitely. But your sister doesn't. She thinks everyone is all lollipops and rainbows. She plans to talk to him later today."

Wilder was quiet. "How old is this guy?"

"Don't know. Mid- to late-fifties maybe." What did that matter?

"You don't think Caley is romantically involved with him, do you? That that's why she's so gung ho on his innocence?" Wilder asked.

Shep's gut clenched. "No."

"Mentorship can slip into hero worship, which can lead to a romantic relationship or denial of any wrongdoing on the mentor's part."

Shep rolled his eyes. "Let me guess. You've been talking with our resident headshrinker, Cosette."

"Well, she's right. It happens. It could be happening to my sister."

Shep scratched the back of his neck. "She hasn't acted like there's anything more than mentorship."

"But she's naive, Shep. You basically said it yourself."

No. What he'd said was that she saw the best in people which made her vulnerable, not naive. "I think it's platonic, dude."

"Good. She deserves a stand-up guy who will treat her right and not take advantage of her. And I plan to be the wall he'll have to tear down to get to her. *If* there's anyone good enough out there for her." He chuckled. "Anything else?"

That description didn't define Shepherd in the least. And even Wilder knew it. Not that Shep would pursue anything. He wouldn't. But if he tried, Wilder would be a wall he'd never get through; he knew too much of Shepherd's old, rowdy ways. The scores of women he loved and left before they could leave him. A heaviness like pitchy tar oozed over his skin and he shuddered, working to forget the past. He wasn't that man anymore.

Time to jam it down, like a jack-in-the-box. Shep could hide his regrets in deep places, but over time the crank would turn until it all popped out unexpectedly, scaring him half to death before Shep shoved it back down again. His vicious cycle to live. Being here with Caley seemed to turn the crank faster.

"I'm going to call Tom and have him look into Leo Fines. I don't trust him," Shepherd said, changing the subject.

"Keep me posted. I don't trust him either. And if he's double-dealing, then I don't want my sister near him. Don't let her around him alone. Just in case."

"I'll stay on her six."

"Yeah, not too close, bro." He chuckled again.

Shep gritted his teeth.

"I'm kidding."

Was he?

"I know you aren't going there."

Of course not. That would be ridiculous. "I'm not interested in anything other than keeping your sister out of harm's way."

"Right. And for as long as it takes, right? Because I'm still tied up and so is everyone else."

Meaning Shep could kiss his cruise bon voyage. "It's fine." He'd already vowed to do whatever it took for as long as it took. He was determined to protect Caley. He'd get it right.

"I'm sorry. I thought she was being paranoid. I can get Wheezer on the computer analysis end. See what turns up on Leo Fines."

Wheezer had once been a major hacker for the wrong team. He could find things that someone in the TBPD might not be able to.

"Once this is over, I really mean it, man. A new cruise. A week longer than you originally planned. On me."

"I'm holding you to it."

"Is Caley around to talk to?" Wilder asked.

"She's inside with Miss Whittle. Getting her settled."

"What'd the doc say about her? Sweet old lady. Met her a time or two."

"Nothing broken. Just bruised up. Came into the kitchen to make tea after a nap. Before she knew it, she was knocked down. Hit her head on the counter. Concussion but heart looks good. They only kept her last night."

"How did she not hear someone trashing the place?"

"Hearing aids weren't in for the nap. Her bedroom is off the kitchen so she didn't see the living room."

"Good. It could have been so much worse if she had."

"Yeah. I guess Caley will want to clean the house up, and she wants to go to Fines with these other occurrences. She thinks he'll change his tune. I'm interested to hear his thoughts." He might not be so much corrupt as he is selfish—wanting to save his own hide at the expense of finding justice for Mary Beth and for Caley's well-being. Both motives disgusted Shep.

"I've got to go. I'll call you when I get a chance. In the meantime, failure is not an option, Shep. This is my baby sister."

"Roger that, Flynn."

He could not—would not—fail.

# FOUR

"Miss Whittle, can I get you anything? Tea? Ice pack? Your knitting?" Caley asked as Miss Whittle shifted in the bed. Thankfully, this room hadn't been destroyed. Which meant whoever was in the house knew Miss Whittle wouldn't have anything that belonged to Mary Beth. Caley's room had been trashed, and her office even more so, which meant they believed she had something worth hurting—or killing—over. Her heart slammed against her ribs, but she worked to mask the fear for Miss Whittle.

"No, hon. I'm tired, is all. A bump to the head will do that." She gave a thin-lipped smile. "Times like this make me miss JC. He wouldn't have let some ruffian in the house. And he sure wouldn't have let someone knock me down." Her smile spread wider at the mention of her husband, bringing sunshine to her lovely face. She was a firm believer in the pink-colored moisturizer. It had paid off. She didn't look her age at all.

"He was a pilot, wasn't he?"

"An ace. In the Korean War. Not everyone gained that kind of status. But my JC was special. Tough as nails. Soft inside. And handsome. Oh, just look." She pointed to the dresser. Several black-and-white photos of her late husband.

"He was a looker for sure." Caley browsed the photos.

"I'm sorry this happened, Miss Whittle. I can't apologize enough but Shepherd is here now and he won't let anyone hurt you again."

Miss Whittle smoothed her quilt. "I believe it. He reminds me of my JC. Grit and goodness. Nothing like a man full of those two ingredients."

Caley chuckled. "I'm going to start the cleanup process. Mrs. Amberly said she'd come by later to sit with you while I run some errands. The gala is coming up and I have a ton of work to do."

"I appreciate your looking after me. Do what you need to, hon. I'll be okay. Good Lord's with me. Always and no matter what." She placed a bony hand on her chest, toying with the gold cross she wore. A symbol of her strong faith.

Caley slipped out and into the living room. Shep hauled a black industrial-sized garbage bag to the street. They'd managed to straighten the living room. She'd started on her bedroom, but it was all so overwhelming. She hadn't noticed anything missing.

But what would they want?

She had nothing of Mary Beth's.

Caley needed to get the office in order. After the intruder's grand display, Shep had declared the futon his new place to bunk until…when? He'd canceled his cruise, which Caley hated, but at the same time, she didn't want to be alone.

He opened the front door and wiped his brow with his corded forearm. He hadn't shaved and his scruff gave him a rugged edge. "How's Miss Whittle?"

"Good considering." She laid her hands on her hips. "You talk to Wilder?"

"Yep."

Caley waited a beat for further information.

None came.

"And?" she prompted.

"And he's going to do some stuff on his end while we work things out on ours." He ran his tongue over his pearly whites. His front left tooth was only slightly shorter than the right, his bottom row uneven. Unlike Caley, who had gone through three years of braces to correct some small shifts in her teeth. But perfectly straight teeth wouldn't fit Shepherd. He was unique down to his minor crooked teeth.

"What's the matter?" He did the Clint Eastwood squint.

How many times would he catch her gawking? It was hard not to. She fiddled with a button on her shirt. "Nothing. Why?"

Cocking his head, he searched her eyes, working to ferret out the truth. She held firm until he grunted and scanned the room.

*Phew.* "I'd like to get the office back in working order. I'll need to work from here more often until Miss Whittle is better. But I do have to give a tour of the facility today, make a few calls regarding the upcoming gala and I have patients to see."

"Turtles?"

"Yes. We logged four stranded turtles two days ago. They're suffering from SCUD." Poor creatures. "But it's treatable with a course of antibiotics. I want to check on them. Ten more days and I can release them." Best part of her job.

"What's SCUD? Because when you say that I think missile."

She hid a smirk. "Of course you do, soldier." She motioned for him to follow her to the office. They could walk and talk. And work and talk. Although Caley was hyperaware that she'd carry the bulk of the conversation.

Inside the office, she kicked at the debris. "SCUD is short for septicemic cutaneous ulcerative disease."

"I like SCUD."

She laughed. It was much easier to remember. She piled books that had been knocked from the shelf into her arms while Shep went to task collecting papers and files and stacking them on her desk.

"It's basically skin rot. Which can be deadly to turtles. And for some reason I'm seeing more of it this year than ever before. Usually, I see maybe two turtles all year with it."

Shep moved swiftly. Even when his body wasn't moving, it was obvious the wheels in his head were. Never still. Caley had studied the way he observed everything from the content of the bookshelves to the way Miss Whittle made tea. Observing wasn't just part of being a solider; no, it was all Shepherd. Maybe he'd been forced to scrutinize things and people in his years as a foster child to protect himself. The thought that he might have never been safe to play or be oblivious broke her heart a little.

"Why turtles?" he suddenly asked. "You read a book or something as a kid?"

What he meant was why not some sort of law enforcement. Even Meghan had worked in a crime lab. Caley hesitated, but he'd stopped cleaning and had given her his undivided attention. Which was saying something for a man who could split his attention in a dozen different directions at once and still keep up.

"When I was seven, my grandpa was killed in the line of duty. Armed robber at a gas station." She shook her head. Gramps had been her world. "I don't know if seven-year-olds can be depressed, but I think I was. Or simply drowning in grief. It was summer and we'd buried him a few weeks earlier. One afternoon, I was sitting by the pool, not even swimming, just dangling my feet and... Meghan brought me a turtle from the pond."

"You made him a pet?"

Caley blinked back tears. She missed Gramps every

day. And Meghan. "No. That's what Meghan suggested. To make me feel better. But I thought putting the turtle in a box would be like putting Gramps in the casket. I didn't like that—seeing him in a casket. Trapped in a box. And I didn't want to do that to the turtle."

Shep cocked his head, held her gaze so intensely she thought he might be able to pull the rest of the story straight from her mind. It alarmed her and sent an uncontrollable spark through her middle.

"I know that sounds strange. He was gone."

"No, it doesn't. And…you were seven."

Caley adjusted her glasses. "I walked down to the pond, studying the markings on his back. The designs mesmerized me and for the first time since he died, I wasn't sad or thinking of Gramps. I was saving a turtle from a casket. I knelt down in the mud, placed him on the bank and waited."

"Did he go into the water?"

"Yeah. After a while. He inched in, submerged and then he came back up. And I tell you…he looked at me. Like he was saying thanks. And I knew then all I'd ever want to do is study and rescue turtles."

Every day as she worked, she carried a part of Gramps. And Meghan.

"Probably sounds weird to you," she said.

"No. Not weird at all." Shep graced her with a half-cocked grin and resumed cleaning. Caley had never shared that story before.

Strange how easy it was to talk to him. Especially when he didn't really talk back much. "What about you, Shep?" She wanted him to, though. "Why did you choose the marines?"

"I wasn't a fan of the navy." His face remained stoic, but she caught it. In his eyes. A small, quick measure of teasing. She'd remember that face. In case he ever joked again.

"Don't you let Wilder hear that," she teased back. Guess he wasn't going to open up. Disappointment sat on the edge of her heart, but Shep wasn't that kind of guy.

"I can take Wilder."

"I—" She was going to say she doubted that. But she wasn't so sure. Wilder might have an inch on Shepherd at six-three, but Shep had an edge with his intense observation skills. He'd be able to anticipate Wilder's moves, and he might have a few extra pounds of muscle, but not much. Also, Wilder might kill her if he knew she was rooting for Shepherd Lightman and not her big brother. "I'm sure you'd give him a good run for his money."

"I'd leave him bankrupt." Another tease. It was in the eyes.

She giggled as they continued to clean the office and reorganize it. Afterward, Caley straightened her bedroom while Shep went out and brought a late lunch in for them and Miss Whittle. Mrs. Amberly arrived an hour later with an old black-and-white movie starring Clark Gable, and Caley and Shep drove to the center.

Before she got out of the car, Shep shifted in his seat. "You need to be prepared for Fines not to respond the way you're anticipating."

"He may not see the connection between Mary Beth's death and her dorm room, but now that my house has been ransacked and my tank tampered with—because I believe it has—he won't deny that they have to be linked."

"And if he does?" Shep asked.

"Then I don't know. But he's not tied to any of it. If I know anything, I know that." Caley stepped from the car.

"He was too quick to dismiss you and your theory. I don't get a good feeling about him." Shep walked her to the entrance.

Granted, she didn't like the way he brushed it off initially either. He'd been thinking of their careers—of his career—and it needled her, but he wasn't a murderer. Shep hadn't been here six months ago when the media had skewed everything about their turtle rehabilitation, slandering their work until it gained the attention of animal protestors who spent two weeks picketing the center. Nora Simms had been fit to be tied and threatened their jobs.

"Mary Beth's death was a blow to us all. He's had time to process everything now. I think you'll find he's not the man you first met." She marched into the center, Shep on her tail. Familiar smells of the briny ocean and bleach from the floors flooded her senses. She loved this job. Losing it would kill her.

Sweeping the truth under the rug would also kill her. Mary Beth deserved justice.

A crowd was touring. Toby Anders, a tech in the lab, showered the group with fun facts and information about turtles. It always warmed her heart to see the enthusiasm among tourists. The fact that they showed up proved they cared about the animals. About the ecosystem. About marine life.

She walked through the center, Shep beside her, waved at the two girls working the information booth, then strode through the employees-only door. A long hallway was lined with offices on the left and a large marine lab with glass windows on the right. At the end of the hall was the door to the equipment room.

Dr. Fines's office was next to hers. Last one on the left. She knocked and received an irritated invitation to enter. She glanced at Shep. As usual he scowled. They entered together and Dr. Fines frowned, but he stood and extended his hand to Shep. "I don't believe we've formally met."

"Shepherd Lightman."

"Caley's friend who's investigating the accident?" He ran his hands through his salt-and-pepper hair.

"It's not an accident, Leo. There have been some new developments." Caley placed her palms on Leo's desk and leaned forward. "My oxygen tank was tampered with yesterday and someone ransacked my home. Like Mary Beth's dorm room. My landlord was hurt."

"I'm sorry to hear about your landlord, Caley." Leo rubbed his chin. "How do you know someone tampered with your tank?" She explained what happened.

"Has the dive expert confirmed your theory?" Leo asked.

"Not yet. We should be hearing back soon, but I've done over four hundred dives. That wasn't a random glitch."

"Maybe not. But you don't know that yet." Leo's lips pursed.

He was being cautious in case the tank's messing up was a fluke. But... "Why would someone trash my house on the heels of doing the same thing to Mary Beth's room? Someone is looking for something."

Leo sat in his leather chair and swiveled it, staring out the window. "Like what?"

Excellent question. "Who knows?"

"Have you shared these new developments with anyone else?" he asked.

"You mean Nora Simms?" How could he be so self-absorbed right now? He was her mentor. Didn't he care about her? About Mary Beth? "No. But we have a—"

"Hunch that this thing is going to keep going sideways, and if it escalates, it's going to get out there," Shep said. Why hadn't he let her inform Leo they had a police contact on the inside? That might put Leo's nerves at ease.

Leo studied Shep, then looked at Caley. "Do you know for sure that these break-ins are connected?"

"My gut says so."

"Your gut." His tone carried frustration and irritation. "Caley, listen to me carefully. If you press this…if the media gets wind of any of this…if Nora does…everything we stand for, everything we've worked for is down the tubes. We can't take a financial hit. We need every donor we have and new ones. And we need this grant."

Caley stole a peek at Shep. Eyes like steel.

"Leo, I can't ignore what has happened. And I don't understand why you are." She folded her arms, hoping for a good answer.

Leo pinched the bridge of his nose. "I'm sorry, Caley. I'm stressed. Having your friend here is going to stir up talk. Turtle Bay is a small community. Someone is bound to figure out who he is and put two and two together or spin their own false tale."

They didn't have time to worry about false tales. They had a dead intern and a killer on the loose who was determined to come after her. How much longer until he raised the stakes to get what he wanted?

Shep leaned forward and down to get at eye level with Leo. "Until I know Caley is safe—because clearly I'm the only one around here who actually cares for her safety—I'm not leaving. I don't care if rumors abound. Used to those anyway. Someone tried to scare her at best or take a shot on her life at worst. You have a dead intern. Two places tossed. Turn a blind eye for the sake of your life's work. Suits me. We don't need your permission, pal." He bored a hole into Leo that would make a shark shiver.

Leo opened his mouth and his cell rang. He glanced down and scowled. "I have to take this. And it's private."

"Said everything that needed saying." Shep saluted and strode to the door, where he waited for Caley.

"Leo, this isn't you. What's going on?"

"Hello," he answered his phone. "Hold on." He covered the speaker. "For your own good, stop meddling. Please."

"What does that mean?" she demanded.

"It means Nora has the power to get you blackballed. You'll never have a career again. Never get another grant no matter where you work," he whispered.

"Well, so be it then. Because finding the truth about Mary Beth's death means more to me than that and it should mean more to you."

He pointed to the phone. "I have to take this. See yourself out."

Caley gaped. "I can't believe you. I don't…I don't even know you." Her heart ached and fire raced through her bones. She stepped into the hallway and held back tears.

Could Shep have been right all along? Could Leo Fines know something about what was happening? And if so, how deep in was he?

Shep wasn't a fan of Leo Fines. The man was at the top of his suspect list, so the last thing he wanted was Caley telling him they had a police detective unofficially investigating. And even if he wasn't in on these attacks, he was still a class-A jerk for hurting Caley. She'd been devoted to him. Loyal. And he'd crushed her in that office.

After the conversation, Caley had mentioned she needed to be alone and walk the beach. Shep had watched from a distance, his Sig Sauer in hand. An hour later, she'd returned and worked on the gala event until her phone rang.

"Hello? Hey, Sal, hold on I'm gonna put you on speaker." She put him on speaker and mouthed, *Scuba expert.* "Well?" she asked.

"I'd like to say it was a freak occurrence, but it wasn't."

Shep wasn't surprised. Caley slumped in her chair.

"The spring in the valve on the top of the cylinder was tampered with. Someone put a little pin in it."

Caley squeezed her eyes shut and chomped her lower lip.

"Which was smart because to tamper with anything else wouldn't make a hill of beans, not with the tank you own."

What did that mean? Shep could dive but he wasn't up on newer equipment or dive technology. He snapped to get Caley's attention.

She opened her eyes and sat up in her chair.

He shook his head.

"I have a friend with me. You're on speaker and he's looking at me weirdly. Let me explain it to him." She turned to Shep. "My tank is designed so that if anything were to malfunction I'd actually get more air, not less. A free flow. But by putting a pin in the valve on the top of the cylinder, it made it appear fine until I dived. As I used the air, the cylinder pressure decreased and then the pin just shut the valve down at some point."

Shep balled his fists. "And you're sure that's what happened?"

"I'm looking at the pin right now," Sal said.

Someone had taken a direct shot at Caley. Heat filled his belly and burned clear to his head. Whoever did this would be found. Shep wouldn't stop until he reached the culprit.

"Thanks, Sal." She hung up. "Well, now what? Do we march into Leo's office with this hard evidence? Make him face the truth, shake him out of denial?"

Denial? Is that what Caley thought was going on? When would she wake up and see Leo Fines was concealing something? What if he was Mystery Man? An affair with an intern would be terrible for his career. But how to reveal his suspicions to Caley without her coming unglued? She was angry with Leo, but didn't seem to suspect him of anything other than being too wrapped up in his career.

It was Caley's career too, but she cared more about Mary Beth than turtles. Her story about falling in love with them had shifted another portion of his heart. He hadn't expected that either.

"Fines isn't interested in the evidence." And if he was connected, Shep wasn't going to continue to update him on their findings. "But we do need to call Detective Tom Kensington with the newest developments and let him work the other end of this. He can print the tank, though I doubt we'll get any prints other than the ones that should be on it." Especially if the interns and staff rotated putting oxygen in the tanks. Someone smart wouldn't leave their prints on the pin in the valve spring. "I'll make the call."

"I can't believe Leo would ignore lives that were supposed to mean something to him to protect his career. I love this job too. I don't want to lose it, but I don't want to die! And I don't want Mary Beth's killer to roam free and not pay for his crime."

He smirked. She may not want to be a part of law enforcement like her family, but the passion to protect and seek justice ran deep in her DNA. He admired it. Admired her tenacity. "Then let's figure this out."

"How about over a pound of crab legs and some shrimp scampi." She adjusted her glasses again, a habit he was coming to admire, as well.

"I could eat."

"There's a little place overlooking the ocean. Reasonably priced too." She led the way to Shep's rental car and climbed inside. Her hands flexed and she gnawed her bottom lip.

"Hey," he said.

She glanced at him as she clicked her seat belt into place.

"Stop worrying. I can keep you safe. You have my word." May not seem like much to her, but he meant it. Whatever it cost, he'd do it.

"Is it that obvious? I'm trying to be strong. I keep thinking, 'What would Wilder do? How would Meghan have responded?' She was so brave when that crazy stalker was after her. I don't know what I'd have done. I'm…" She shrugged.

She was what? A weird sensation to take her hand overwhelmed him.

That was new.

He balled his fist instead. He was here to guard her. That's it. The only touching he planned to do was if he needed to toss her out of harm's way. "Little Flynn, I don't know what you were about to say and I'm not one to pry. So I'll just say this. You're risking your life and career to find out who killed Mary Beth and who is coming after you. That's proactive. That's brave." He cranked the engine. "Now fix your glasses, which are drooping off your nose, and give me the coordinates to this crab shack."

She stared at him long enough to make him uncomfortable, then pushed her dark frames into place. "Thanks for the pep talk, Shep. It means a lot coming from you."

He grunted. Compliments weren't his thing either.

Twenty minutes later, they were seated at a table on a dock overlooking the Gulf. Seagulls circled and cawed in a sky devoid of a single cloud. A huge tiki umbrella shielded them from the merciless heat. Tourists with too much sun gathered at nearby tables enjoying a surf-and-turf lunch. The smell of seafood, grilled beef and salt from the ocean wafted on the breeze rolling in.

They ordered soft drinks and Shep toyed with a pack

of crackers on the table. "This is a nice place to live," he commented.

"I think so. It's small. Low crime. Until now." She glanced up when the server brought their sodas and took their order. She sipped hers and toyed with the straw. "You have Leo on the top of your list, don't you?"

Shep laid his elbows on the table and leaned forward, debating how much to say. Might as well get it out there. Let her be mad. "He could be Mystery Man. Makes sense if that theory is true. If we had Mary Beth's phone, we could search it for pictures. It's possible that's what the intruder was after all along. Or text messages that might not have been deleted."

"What if it's not a mystery man? I don't believe Mary Beth would be into drugs. What else could he be looking for? And if he is looking for photos or text messages on a phone, he didn't find them in the dorm room because he ransacked my place. Which means he still hasn't found what he wanted. What if her phone was lost at sea?"

Shep swigged his drink. He should have ordered water. "If it is lost to the ocean, he doesn't know it or he wouldn't have broken into the dorm room or your house."

"If it's not out at sea, where could it be?"

Million dollar question. Unless it had a waterproof case, she wouldn't have taken it swimming or kayaking. She hadn't left it in the dorm room or they would have found it when they packed everything up for Mary Beth's parents.

Could someone have come in, before the intruder broke in, and taken it? That would explain why none of them had found it. But then that would open up a whole new complication. How many people had been after Mary Beth and what she was hiding?

Their food came and Shep's mouth watered at the pile of crab legs, boiled potatoes, baby ears of corn and delicious steak. Caley had opted for shrimp scampi over beef. He cracked open his crab legs and dipped the meat in garlic butter. "Good choice, Little Flynn. This is the stuff."

She grinned and raked her shrimp through the sauce. "Hey, I know my restaurants. I like to eat."

They continued to dig into their meal as they made small talk about the weather and the upcoming gala. Caley shared about Arnold Simms and his life work, tourism in Turtle Bay and where she planned to spend Thanksgiving this year. "I love going home. But it's hard to be there too."

Shepherd had been ripped from his drug addicted mother when he was only eight years old, but he'd been taking care of himself long before that. Seen more of life before the age of six than most adults. Bounced from house to house. Never been able to say he'd loved a single one.

No one ever wanted him enough to adopt. Probably his fault anyway. He'd been like an angry bull busting from the chute. Ready to buck and stomp on anyone who came in striking distance, anyone who tried to tame him. Not a single person could make those eight seconds.

"What will you do for the holiday? Will you be at my parents' house again?"

Thanksgiving? He'd spent the past two with them.

There but distant.

Like feeling the glow of a cozy fire while standing with his nose to a cold glass pane as snow fell.

She finished off her last shrimp and tossed her napkin on her platter.

"I don't know. Wilder owes me a cruise. I may take it over the holidays." He licked the butter off his finger and signaled the server for the check.

"Alone on the holidays? Shep, don't do that."

"Nothing new for me, Little Flynn. No skin off my

teeth." He grabbed the check. Caley tried to snag it from him, but his grip was tighter. "I got this."

"It's the least I can do."

"I'll write it off." He winked.

"Yeah, let's make Wilder pay for it." She giggled, then turned serious. "You don't have to be alone, Shep. Wilder's team is part of his family. And if you're Wilder's family, then you're mine too. And Mama and Daddy's. I'll make you a deal. You go. I'll go."

His heart ached. No words came.

He paid the check and led Caley from the restaurant. What would it be like to truly be part of a family? Not from Wilder's end but Caley's—to be connected to her?

He reined in those thoughts. Thinking of Caley in that way was unacceptable.

She was off-limits romantically. Even if he did grow close to her, she'd want him to open up and share his history. Then she'd walk away.

And Shep didn't let anyone walk out on him anymore. Not since he was sixteen. No, Shep did the leaving before he could become attached and be abandoned. Life worked smoother that way for him. Besides, Wilder had all but spelled out the truth.

Caley Flynn deserved a man with a past full of integrity. A man who would know how to love her properly. A man who wouldn't hurt her.

Or walk out on her.

He opened her car door for her and rounded the hood to the driver's side.

Something in his peripheral caught his attention.

A white van like the one the intruder had jumped into when he'd given Shep the slip at Caley's was parked down the street. He slid into the driver's seat, adjusted his mirror and pulled out onto the small main street. Two lights down, the van was about five car lengths back.

They were being followed.

# FIVE

Caley quietly studied Shep from the corner of her eye. He glanced in the rearview mirror more often. And his *accidental* wrong turn was suspicious.

He was trying to hide the fact that they were being followed.

Nerves popping and stomach knotting, Caley tried to hide her fear, but her palms had turned clammy as she sat on edge.

"I haven't seen all of Turtle Bay. Mind if we take a scenic drive?" Shep asked as he eyed the side mirror.

Her heart hammered in her chest, pounded in her ears. "I'd appreciate it if you wouldn't pull any punches with me, Shepherd."

He skidded a glance her way and dipped his chin. "We've got a tail on us."

Caley gawked in her side mirror. A white van was a few car lengths back. "You have an uncanny ability to see things no one else seems to. So are they just no good or did you use that ability?"

The side of his mouth tipped upward. "I'm astute and they're not that good. I took that wrong turn to see if they'd move on, knowing they'd been made. Guess they haven't realized it yet."

Caley itched to pivot in her seat and try to see faces.

Five lengths back it was all dark, and the driver wore a ball cap pulled low. "Can you lose them?"

He grunted.

"I didn't mean to insult you." She didn't doubt any of Shepherd's skills.

"Just sit back, relax."

*Relax?*

He made a right off the main road and onto a side street in a small subdivision. The van also turned.

He pulled into a random driveway. The van slowed.

Caley's breath hitched.

"Might need you to get down if this goes south," he said, drawing a side piece.

Now she couldn't breathe at all. She undid her seat belt and scooched in the passenger seat.

Seconds ticked by.

The van turned the corner but halted.

*Don't back up. Don't come back!*

Her heart hammered. But Shep kept one hand calmly on the wheel, the other on his gun. He wasn't even breaking a sweat. Unlike Caley. Sweat trickled down her neck, popped on her upper lip. She swiped at it with the back of her hand. "Should we get out of the car? Like we're here to visit?"

"No."

And why not? She waited for an answer. None came.

"Face me like we're talking."

"Okaaaay." She shifted, hated having her back to the van that lurked around the corner.

"We need to look engaged enough that we aren't ready to go inside."

"And why can't we just walk up to the door?"

"Because I don't know if they have a sniper rifle in hand. So you aren't going out in the open."

Ice hit her stomach. Someone might be waiting to pick

her off? Facing Shepherd wasn't going to convince anyone of anything. "Soldier, the only thing that would keep us from going in is physical contact."

Shepherd's eyes widened. "Come again?"

She leaned in, sliding across the console, until she could smell his masculine, understated cologne. Cool. Controlled. And smelling like a glorious dream. She licked her lips.

Shepherd glanced at the van, visibly backed up an inch. "What are you doing, Little Flynn?"

"I'm making them think we have a much better reason not to go inside. Aren't you saying that they might know we've identified that they're following us? If so, then what are they willing to lose? Nothing." Her stomach churned.

Shepherd held her gaze. "I can't kiss you," he whispered.

Disappointment lodged in her chest. So he wasn't attracted to her. Okay. This was for show anyway. No time for her ego to deflate. "I see," she muttered. "It was a dumb idea anyway." Her cheeks heated.

"No, I can't kiss you *and* watch the van at the same time."

Oh.

"So tilt your head to the right." He let his eyes trail from the van to her. "And come here," he breathed as he cupped the back of her neck, tipping his head to the left and running his fingers through her hair.

For a man who didn't do physical contact, he had this down pat.

Her head tingled and she nearly forgot a van sat forty feet away with a possible sniper inside. Gently guiding her toward his lips, he paused an inch from her mouth, his breath deliciously minty and warm.

Tension in the car built and her nerves hummed.

"Can you still see them?" she whispered.

"Mmm-hmm," he rasped.

She nervously slid her hands up his biceps. Powerful like oaks. Her throat turned parched and she could barely swallow, barely breathe. She lifted her chin; her nose brushed his. He flinched.

"Sorry."

"Stop talking." His husky voice sounded strained, and his eyes seemed to darken from blue to gray, then he shifted his gaze from her to the van.

"Sir, yes, sir," she breathed.

His sight flickered back to her, to her lips and then he arrested her eyes before sliding his hand from her hair and heaving a sigh. He leaned back as if he'd never been so relieved to break from a fake kiss. "They're gone. But buckle up. They might be circling the block."

Caley forced herself to slide back to her seat. To shake away the feelings she'd been having. For a moment she thought there might have been a two-sided connection. Apparently not.

Better this way. She didn't kiss men casually. And she wasn't going to let a solider like Shepherd Lightman charge her heart and take it captive. She clicked her seat belt into place.

Shep threw it in Reverse and blew out of there. "Nice call, Little Flynn."

Was it?

"We'll be gone if they swing back by."

She turned the vents toward her and cranked the air-conditioning. "Why are they following us? Do they think I have what they're looking for on my person?"

Shep scanned the mirrors, the roads. "Possible."

He drove across the main street, into another small neighborhood. "There a back way to your bungalow?"

"Yeah." She gave Shep the directions and they made it back to Caley's without the van popping up again. They knew where she lived. Why not camp out there? Why fol-

low her? "You think they might believe what they're looking for is hidden and following us will lead them to it?"

"Possible."

She wanted to scream. Sometimes Shep was too tight-
lipped. An iron wall. Keeping words and emotions hostage. They were going to be in close quarters for who
knew how long. Would he ever open up? She shouldn't
give two hoots if she got to know him on a personal level.
He didn't want to know her on one. She was nothing more
than a mission.

And that rankled.

And the fact that it rankled also rankled.

She wasn't so stupid as to believe Shep was the kind of
guy who had serious relationships. Stories had been told
when she'd been in earshot. Stories of his many flings.
Never kept a woman long. Of course, she'd never seen
any of these women. He'd never brought one to her parents' home. Why would he if they never meant anything?

"Shep, what's the longest you've been in a romantic
relationship?" she asked as they walked to her front door.
She mentally kicked herself.

"What?" His head snapped in her direction.

"You heard me. I'm curious."

"Why?" He narrowed his eyes.

Because she was an idiot setting herself up for heart-
break by getting too close. She shrugged. "I just am."

"I don't know." He shifted from one foot to the other and
massaged the back of his neck. As she unlocked the front
door and stepped into the welcoming air-conditioning, the
smell of cinnamon came from the kitchen. Had Mrs. Amberly baked? She kinda hoped so.

"You don't know? How do you not know?" Would he
ever answer a personal question? "What happened to lay-
ing it on me straight?"

"How is this relevant to the case?"

The case. Confirmed. She was just a mission. "I guess it's not." She smothered her irritation and greeted Mrs. Amberly in the kitchen. Oatmeal raisin cookies had been arranged on a platter. "How's Miss Whittle?"

"Vickie is doing well. She's asleep, so I thought I'd put myself to good use. They're still warm." She pointed to the platter. "Enjoy. If you need me, call. I'm a stone's throw away." She patted Caley's shoulder and nodded politely to Shep, who had entered the kitchen, his presence looming behind her. Tension rippling between them. Uncomfortable tension.

"You like cookies?" Caley asked.

He snagged one. "Yep."

Caley grabbed two. Paused. Took a third. Shep was driving her to new levels of frustration.

"Three weeks," he called.

She froze, slowly turned. Shep's neck was flushed and he scratched above his ear, not meeting her gaze. Not long at all. In college, Caley had dated Jeremy for about a year, but he'd gotten an internship overseas and that was too far for Caley to travel, especially when there hadn't been talk of wedding bells. After that she'd dated some. The last relationship stretched about eight months. But he'd been ready to go to a level Caley wasn't. That's what she got for dating a man who didn't share her faith.

Did Shep?

"Who broke it off?"

"I did."

"Why?"

"It wasn't my thing." He shoved the rest of his cookie in his mouth.

Relationships weren't his thing? Or the woman wasn't? She was afraid to ask. "I'm going to early service at church tomorrow. Would that be your thing?"

"Yeah."

She inhaled. Exhaled. Hoping to relax her coiled muscles. "Do you normally go to church?" She eyed him, willing him to expound with more than the three-word max he seemed to reserve for anything that didn't pertain to the case.

"Every Sunday I'm not working."

An ember of hope cracked loose in her chest. "Really?"

"I'm a Christian, if that's the mountain you're going around." He grabbed another cookie.

"How—"

"We don't need Mary Beth's phone to see what's on it. What kind of cell did she have?"

So he was shutting down the personal conversation. Fine. The case was more important anyway. "An iPhone. I don't know which model."

"We only need access to her iCloud account," he continued. "A girl her age would probably have everything backed up online. I'm gonna call Wheezer and see what he can do to get us in."

Wilder's analyst had been dubbed Wheezer back in grade school because of his asthma. The name had stuck. Poor guy. He didn't seem to mind it, though. "What's his real name?"

Shep pulled out his phone and paused. "I have no idea." He chuckled. "You want me to ask him?"

"No. He might be offended." She bit into her cookie. "I'm going to check on Miss Whittle." And take a break from Shep's presence. She hurried down the hall. Miss Whittle was still asleep. She crammed down cookie number two, went into the living room and curled up on the couch, scrolling through her emails. Nothing about the grants she'd applied for. She should be hearing from at least one of them any day now.

She checked her social media. So Shep was a Christian. That meant different things to each person. To some it meant believing in God and faithfully going to church. For others it meant a personal relationship outside of Sundays. Which was Shep?

Since Meghan died, Caley had fallen somewhere in between. She tapped a Bible app and looked at the daily verse. *Jeremiah* 17:7.

*But blessed are those who trust in the Lord and have made the Lord their hope and confidence.*

Meghan had hoped in the Lord. She'd had confidence. But she was murdered. And that was where Caley struggled most. Having hope and confidence didn't shield God's people from harm. Confidence in Christ didn't equal a spared life.

So what did it mean?

Could she trust God to keep her safe? Could she trust Him to save her life from peril?

There was no guarantee. Otherwise Meghan would be alive.

"Hey."

She jumped. "You scared me."

Shep perched on the edge of her recliner. "Wheezer—whose name is Larry and he prefers Wheezer—said he'll work on getting us into her iCloud account. He'll email us when he has something. Once he's in he can locate her phone, or where it was last before it died. I'd say by now it's dead."

Caley couldn't sit on her hands, but she didn't want to leave Miss Whittle alone. "I'll work on the gala. I've nailed down the catering, seating, music. But I always make a slideshow of our work from the previous year and end it with clips of hatchlings making their way to the ocean."

"How do they know where to go? The turtle babies?"

Caley grinned. Turtle babies. "They're phototactic. Attracted to light. The brightest light guides them. That's why we don't allow vehicles on the beach at night. They can get confused and crawl toward the headlights instead of following the moonlight over the ocean."

"So they die if they go toward the false light?"

Exactly. "They could."

"Reminds me of something biblical," Miss Whittle said as she appeared in the living room, a smile on her face. Color had come back to her cheeks. "The Bible talks about the enemy masquerading as an angel of light. False light. If we get confused and crawl toward it, it can kill us spiritually."

Caley hadn't ever thought of that. But Miss Whittle was right. Being guided by the wrong light could definitely put someone in danger.

"Now. I'm feeling much stronger and more myself. Don't insist on babysitting me. Besides, Mr. and Mrs. Bloom are next door and they know someone broke in. They're on neighborhood watch."

"I'd feel terrible if something else happened, Miss Whittle." Caley couldn't take that chance. Plus they were being followed. Someone could be watching the house even now. As if Shep shared her thoughts, he ambled to the window, peered out.

"Honey, I refuse to live in fear. God didn't create us to do so. Whatever happens, it is well with my soul. My hope is in God."

*God, why can't I have faith like Miss Whittle?*

"She's right, Little Flynn. We're all gonna face our Maker at some point. And I guess it's not so much our end as a new beginning." He glanced at her and smiled at Miss Whittle.

Caley nearly dropped to the floor. Well, that answered her question on how deep Shep's faith went. Maybe that's why he didn't mind rushing into battle from the front line.

"Well said, my boy. Well said. Skedaddle." Miss Whittle left them alone in the living room.

"Who else would have information about Mary Beth?" Shep asked.

"Toby Anders. In the lab."

"Let's go see him."


There weren't enough oatmeal raisin cookies in the world to ease the humiliation searing through Shep. Three weeks. That was the longest relationship he'd been in but somehow he felt he owed Caley a truth about himself.

Her idea about kissing had thrown him for a loop, sending his heart upside down. Then to have her nose right there against his, and her sweet breath on his lips when she spoke... He'd needed her to shut up or he would have made the biggest mistake ever.

Because he'd wanted to kiss her.

But if he was going to keep his head on straight, he couldn't. He had to keep her safe. Kissing was nothing but a distraction. One he wouldn't mind exploring, but Wilder would kill him. Shep would ream himself out.

Because he didn't do long-term relationships.

*Three weeks*.

The subtle shock on Caley's face at those two words had struck a blow, but the look on her face when he'd mentioned meeting God face-to-face was the knockout punch. Shock. Disbelief that a guy like him, with his list of shortcomings, might have faith in God.

Yeah, he had the faith to believe that he was eternally secure. He'd accepted Jesus as his Savior. But he'd yet to come to grips with God being a father. That was a tougher pill to swallow. His own father hadn't bothered to care enough to introduce himself.

He'd studied Wilder and Caley's dad. Mr. Flynn was everything he imagined a dad might be. But he wasn't

Shep's father. And going to holidays at the Flynns' only reminded him of everything he'd been cheated out of. Father-son milestones. Knowing how a man loved a woman and led his family. What if a woman walked out on him because he didn't know how to love her properly? He'd been attracted to women. Dated them. But he'd never experienced being in love with a single one. Never opened the lid on his past. Never even shared a favorite color or food.

Made it easier to leave and he'd never wanted to stay.

So why had he spilled out an embarrassing truth to Caley Flynn of all people? He glanced over. She'd been messing with her nails on the drive to the center. Quiet.

Did she now see him in a different light? A man who couldn't commit to a relationship might not be able to follow through with his commitment to keep her safe. Surely she had to know that wasn't true. He parked in her designated parking space and killed the engine.

"I'm gonna stick this out. See it through to the end."

She raised her chin, peered into his eyes. "I know you will, Shepherd. You're a good soldier."

The way she said *soldier* sent a wave of unease through him. As if it that was a bad word. "And I'm going to make sure you come through it safely."

"I appreciate that. Thank you." So prim. Proper.

He'd marred himself with his admission. Couldn't change it. He regretted telling her. Inside, she strode to her office and opened her mini fridge, pulling out a can of peach tea. "You want anything? I have this and water."

"Pass."

She cracked open the can and swigged. "Don't tell my mama."

He grinned; she seemed more herself. "Secret's safe with me." Tea in a can. "Don't let all the South bleed out of ya, though."

"Never." She sighed. "It's actually really good."

"Again. Pass."

"Let's go find Toby." She locked her office door and they scurried down the hall to the lab. Toby was a gangly kid with a breakout flaring on his cheeks.

"Hey, Caley."

"Toby. How goes it?" Caley looked at Shep. "This is my friend Shepherd Lightman."

Toby gave him a clammy, weak handshake. "Nice to meet you."

"I wanted to talk to you about Mary Beth." Caley laid a hand on his lanky arm. "Did she confide in you about anything? Or did she act odd in the weeks before she died?"

Toby rubbed his brow with his forearm. "Confide like what?"

"Was she seeing anyone other than Billy?" Caley asked.

"No," Toby said. "Not that I know of. But she was going to break things off with him. He would swing by the lab 'bout every day and then in the last week or so it stopped. I asked her about it."

"And?" Caley prompted.

Toby shifted, kept glancing at Shepherd. "Said that she wasn't sure they were going to work out, but when she didn't offer any more information I didn't pry."

Caley nodded. "And what about her behavior?"

Toby's mouth twisted from one side to the other and he stared toward the wall. "Well, she did seem to be obsessed with the logbooks."

"What logbooks?" Shep asked.

Caley turned. "We have the interns and some volunteers log when turtles nest and lay their clutch, and we count them. It's a lot of work, depending on the species of turtle. There can be fifty to two hundred eggs. But it's important so we get it done."

"We also log how many turtles we rescue and when

we release them. Where we found them. Data like that," Toby offered.

"Which logs was she obsessed with?" Shep asked.

Toby pointed to the filing cabinet. "Egg count. Turtle logs."

Caley beelined it to the filing cabinet. "Recent ones?"

"I guess." Toby rubbed his hands on his cargo shorts. "You don't think her death was accidental, do you?"

"We're just looking into every angle." Shep studied Caley as she loaded her arms with logbooks. "Why isn't your data digitalized?"

"It is. We keep both. We log with paper. Then add the extra measure of entering into the system. Leo is old-school and we don't need all those tablet lights out on the beach." Caley handed Shep the stack of logbooks. "Thanks, Toby. Keep this quiet, will you?"

Toby nodded emphatically. "No problem."

Back in Caley's office, Shep dropped the logbooks on her desk. "What are we looking for?"

"I have no idea. But if she was obsessing over something in one of these entries, then I want to know it. It might be what got her killed." Caley swigged the rest of her peach tea and shot it in the trash can.

Shep opened a journal. Location of each nest, number of eggs in the nest, what species of turtle. A check mark had been placed if the eggs had hatched along with the date of the hatch. "If she found something odd in the logbooks, we ought to, as well, right? A discrepancy of some kind? Question is how will we find it? You only do initial counts of the eggs."

She ignored him as she engrossed herself in one of the journals, then she rummaged through them, a frown on her face.

"What's the problem?"

She shook her head. "I'm missing three weeks of rehabilitation and rescue journals." She went to work clacking on her keyboard. "The information hasn't been entered yet. Where would three weeks of journal entries have disappeared to?"

"Maybe that's what the intruder is looking for." Incriminating information could be in those journals. Like missing turtles.

Caley's eyes widened. "You don't think someone on the inside is stealing turtles do you?"

She was following his thinking. If Mary Beth had found a discrepancy in the logbooks, she might have gone to someone who didn't want that information known. "Sea turtles are a delicacy overseas. I've been to Thailand. Seen it. And they're used for medicinal purposes, as well. A lot of money can be made, Caley."

Her cheeks drained of color and she jumped up. "I'm going to Leo."

"We discussed this." Leo wasn't innocent. Going to him with these accusations might send him over the edge, and Caley's life was at stake. "You can't go in with information you don't have, Little Flynn. What proof is there that this might be going down?"

She tapped a finger on one of the journals and her color came back to her cheeks. "I won't go in accusing, but keeping up with the journals and entries is my job. Inquiring about a few missing journals isn't accusing."

Excellent point. Shep would like to see his reaction. "Okay."

Caley stormed out the office door and blew into Leo's office. He raised his head, brow knit.

"I'm missing three weeks' worth of logs." She folded her arms and pinned Dr. Fines with a hard glare. So much for not accusing him of anything.

"I have them. Why is that a problem?"

"Why do you have them?"

Leo's eyebrows rose. "Because I run this facility and I'm gathering some private data. Like I always do. Getting ready for my presentation to donors. I need statistics and numbers." He frowned. "And since when do you barrel into my office like this?"

She heaved a breath. "Since you decided to ignore the fact that someone killed Mary Beth and attacked me."

Fines glanced away. Guilty? "I'm sorry, Caley, that you feel I'm insensitive. I'm not. I've called and checked on the Whalings and sent flowers on behalf of our center."

Big deal. This guy was hiding something. An affair with Mary Beth. Something sinister to do with the turtles. Or something they hadn't come across yet.

"Can I see the logbooks?" Caley asked.

"When I'm done with them and have my PowerPoint all together, of course." He held her gaze.

Finally, Caley backed down. "You can leave them on my desk." She turned and strode back to her office. For a while she didn't speak, but the turmoil in her eyes said it all. She was awakening to the fact that her mentor and boss might be the bad guy.

"Caley," he murmured.

"Yeah?"

"It's time to be more proactive. To do some surveillance on Leo Fines. I don't trust him." Shep waited for her permission but he was doing it regardless.

She opened another can of peach tea, but instead of drinking it, she traced circles along the outside of the can. "I'm going with you. I need to see for myself. Because… because I can't believe Leonard Fines might be a criminal of some kind."

Shep did surveillance best alone. "Not a good idea. It could be dangerous and I don't want to purposely put you in the line of fire if it goes sideways." Wilder would kill him, for one. Not to mention he didn't want to get into a predicament that might require fake kissing again. Because fake kissing might not stay pretend.

"It's tailing him. How much danger can we end up in?"

Questions like that should never be asked. Whoever was out there was desperate. And willing to murder.

Anything could go wrong.

# SIX

Shep hung back as Caley injected antibiotics into some of the sick sea turtles. Her gentle ways mesmerized him. Wilder would have Shep's hide if he knew the thoughts rolling around in his mind concerning his baby sister. None inappropriate, but he was entertaining the idea of having her in his arms, of feeling her lips on his or even strolling down the beach holding hands.

Where was this coming from? Holding hands wasn't his thing. Strolling a beach wasn't something Shepherd did, for that matter. But he could picture it. With Caley. Her slender fingers laced with his rough ones.

Her glasses had slipped down her nose again and her wild mass of hair was all over the place on her head, yet it seemed strategically placed that way. Did she have any clue how incredibly beautiful she was? If so, she never flaunted it.

An email notification dinged on his phone and he checked it. Wheezer. He didn't want to interrupt Caley's work, but she'd want to see this. Mary Beth's iCloud account had been accessed, and he had all of her information. Photos. Videos. The whole enchilada.

"There there, you sweet thing," Caley cooed. "You'll be back to your world before you know it." She ran her hands over its shell and caught Shep staring. "Releasing them is the best. Next week, I'll be able to do that. If you're here, you can come along."

He'd like that. A lot.

"I have an email from Wheezer."

Caley cleared her throat. "You got it from here, Toby?"

"Sure."

She excused herself and they went into her office. Shep used Caley's computer to open his email and download the photos. Several group photos of the interns arriving at the center. More with Caley. With turtles. Friends. Random scenery. At a park. Lots of them at a park.

"She loved Palm Park. It's on the north end of Turtle Bay. Good for bird and alligator watching. And just enjoying Florida's beauty."

He continued flipping.

Mary Beth and Billy Reynolds.

Mary Beth and Ashley.

Mary Beth and Toby. Hmm… "What do you make of this one?"

Caley studied the photo. "Friends taking a selfie. Everyone does it."

"Check her Instagram. Did she post it on there?" The photo was innocent in and of itself. His arm slung around her shoulder while she leaned into him and smiled for the camera. But his eyes… Something was in the eyes. "Isn't he engaged?"

"Yes. To a girl back home. He's from Clearwater. Sees her on weekends." Caley scrolled through Mary Beth's Instagram. "I don't see it, but that doesn't mean they were in a secret romantic relationship."

They might not have been.

But then, they might have. Shepherd couldn't rule any possibility out.

By the time they scrolled through the last one, frustration had coiled the muscles around Shep's shoulders and neck. No Mystery Man. Unless it was Toby. Nothing of her and Leo that didn't include the other interns. He checked his watch. 1830 hours.

Rustling from outside drew his attention. He cracked open the door. Leo was locking up his office and leaving for the day. "He's on the move. Let's go." The past few days, they'd tailed him, but he hadn't gone anywhere other than the office, home and occasionally the grocery store. Shepherd hadn't even seen his wife once. Seemed odd. Were they on the outs? If so, was it because he was Mystery Man?

Caley scrambled from her chair and grabbed her purse while Shep waited for the sound of footsteps to disappear. Reopening the door, Shep peered out and motioned Caley to follow. Leo headed to his silver Avalon. They hurried to Shep's rental car and waited for Leo to leave. When he turned onto the main street, Shep left the parking lot, staying more than five cars behind.

"You said Fines was married, right? Not divorced?" Shepherd asked.

"Why? Are you still thinking he's Mystery Man? He's not. He's a happily married man with a daughter he dotes on, who happens to be a year older than Mary Beth, so to insinuate he was having an affair with Mary Beth grosses me out completely."

"It's possible, though."

"I'm not naive. I know things like that happen."

Just not to Leo Fines is what she didn't add.

He turned onto Tourist Row. Restaurants. Clubs. Tattoo shops. "Well, this isn't home."

Caley shifted in her seat. "No. It's not."

Leo's car turned down an alley in between two tall buildings.

"We can't take the car down there. I'm going to slip out and go on foot." He unbuckled and opened his door.

"I am too then."

"No. Stay put."

Caley removed her seat belt. "If he's into something bad, I want to see it with my own eyes."

Looking into watery, desperate eyes, Shep couldn't deny her this. Against his better judgment, he caved. The woman did things to him. Softened him. He'd have to pull it together. "Fine, but stay on my six."

"Yes, sir." She slipped out of the car and they stuck close to the stucco buildings. As they slunk around the corner of one of the buildings—a club—Leo Fines climbed out of his car, a dark duffel bag in hand.

"That doesn't look like an innocent man, Little Flynn." Shep hated to disappoint her. But this guy was crooked. Shep looked at the sign hanging on the back door. The Nest. "What's the skinny on this place? You know?"

"It's been in the papers before. Fights. Gets pretty rowdy at times. Some of the interns blow off steam here on weekends." Caley chewed her thumbnail. "What do you think is in that bag?"

Fines knocked and the door opened. A man with tree trunks for biceps and a shiny noggin stepped out and motioned Fines inside. "Nothing good." He retrieved his phone and took a picture.

Caley softly groaned. "That's what I was afraid of."

Shep inched along the side of the building, then darted behind a Dumpster, Caley right on his tail. The smell of days-old trash hit his gag reflex. Flies buzzed.

He snapped a few more pictures of Fines's car and the building before him, then he scrolled through the pictures in Mary Beth's iCloud account while they waited. One seemed familiar. There. Same bright yellow stucco. A neon sign with a wave on it. The Nest. "Mary Beth has been here." He showed Caley the photo. "You know who she might have been with? It's just a photo of the place. I don't see anyone from your center in it."

Caley studied the photo. "No. Mary Beth didn't go to clubs."

"Well, someone took this picture with her phone. I think she's been here even if she didn't go inside." Question was…*why?* And what was in Fines's duffel bag? Money? Couldn't be turtles. Those things were huge. But maybe smaller ones. Like hatchlings.

A few minutes later, Fines came out without the bag. Shep snapped another photo.

When he drove off, Shep turned to Caley. Her eyes pooled. "I'm sorry." It sickened him that the man she'd looked up to for so long was corrupt at best. Possibly a murderer behind the tampering of Caley's oxygen tank.

She nodded and slipped her glasses off, swiped at her eyes and put the glasses back on. "Me too."

"We need to poke around inside that club." Someone inside might have known Mary Beth. Or maybe they could actually discover what was worth murdering her for.

"Well, it is Saturday night," Caley said. "We can go in under the guise of club hopping on the weekend. Although, I seriously doubt someone will have turtles out for sale."

"No. But she had a picture of that club for a reason. Leo was inside. This place has something to do with her death. My gut says so."

"Mine too."

"I'll call Tom at Turtle Bay Police Department and see what inside information he has on this club." He motioned for her to head back to the car. She darted from behind the Dumpster, Shep following. He glanced up at the window overlooking the alley, and a curtain shifted.

Had they been spotted?

* * *

Caley finished applying her makeup. She rarely wore it, but they were going undercover and she had to look the part. She'd dressed in trendy jeans, a flowy black blouse and black wedges. She straightened her hair, left it down and gave her eyelids a smoky effect with charcoal and soft gray shadows. What exactly had they seen at the club earlier? Could Shep's suspicions be true? Could Leo be a part of something as vile as selling turtles? What else could it be? She hadn't had the chance to look into the logs. Leo still had them.

And how would they figure it out tonight? As if someone would be set up in a booth auctioning off sea turtles. But if anyone could sniff out something nefarious, it was Shep with his sixth sense. She was counting on it. Each day zapped her strength. Worry ran in her veins. Until they figured out the truth, Caley was in danger. The thought lodged in her throat, but she swallowed it down, spritzed a light perfume in the air and walked through it.

She hadn't been this dressed up since her last date with a professor from the University of Tampa. It hadn't ended well. Her nerves hummed. Did she look okay? Would Shep think so? Not that it mattered since this wasn't a date. Shep wasn't interested in her and she shouldn't be interested in him. But she couldn't deny that she was.

The man was a mystery. She wanted to pry her way in and see what was buried underneath that tough exterior, dig past the soldier to the man. Who was Shepherd Lightman really? What if she did get past the rough edges and found he was a man she very much could love? How long would she have him before he left her? Before he wandered into a deadly mission and it got him killed, leaving her devastated and mourning like Gran. Never to recover. Never to be the same.

No. She wouldn't let it happen.

She smoothed her hair and glanced one last time in the mirror. This eye shadow made her blue eyes pop. Taking a deep breath, she opened the bedroom door and tiptoed toward the sounds in the kitchen.

Shep stood with his back to her.

Caley's knees buckled and she nearly fanned her face with her hand.

No longer was he in his signature jeans and black or white T-shirt.

He'd traded all that in for stylish faded jeans that fit him just right and a dressy white shirt that clung to his muscular back and biceps. Wide cuffs met his elbows, revealing corded forearms, and accented his tanned skin.

She cleared her throat.

"You ready to—" He turned and the rest of his statement died on his lips. He stood, mouth open.

Her stomach knotted. "Shep?"

He took his sweet time scanning her from head to toe before meeting her with a gaze that completely baffled her. "I'm gonna have to break an arm tonight. I can see it already," he muttered.

"Excuse me? I thought we were there to do surveillance or something, not manhandle folks."

"Manhandling is going to be unavoidable, I'm afraid. Little Flynn, you're not looking so little right now." He blew a heavy breath and rubbed his ear, then breezed past her.

Excitement rippled down her spine and warmed her insides. Shepherd Lightman had seen her as something other than a mission. A woman. Unfortunately, it couldn't move past attraction for either of them. She met him in the living room. "It's after eight. You ready?"

"Yes and no." Now he seemed irritated.

Had she done something wrong? They were supposed to go to a club. She'd dressed up. Completely appropriate dress attire for that matter. The man was confusing to say the least. "I'm going to let Miss Whittle know we'll be out late."

He responded with a grunt and now he wouldn't look at her. After she said her goodbyes, they drove to the club and parked across the street in the open lot. Music blared. Cigarette smoke, beer and a mixture of perfumes and colognes saturated the muggy air.

The grill two buildings down reminded Caley they hadn't eaten. Paying the cover charge, they entered the crowded nightclub.

Neon lights flashed as a DJ spun records. The bass was so loud it thumped in Caley's chest. A railing surrounding an open mezzanine on the second floor popped in neon pink. A sleek black bar ran the length of the west wall. Four guys served drinks to the flood of patrons packed in like sardines.

Suddenly Caley was uncomfortable. The kind of partying going on here had never been her scene. She'd given her life to Jesus in first grade and had never gone through a rebellious stage. She licked her lips and willed herself to try to look at ease. Like she belonged.

She glanced at Shep. A huge grin spread across his face as he subtly moved to the music, his eyes taking in the surroundings, the people. He seemed to fit, but on closer inspection, behind that facade, Caley recognized discomfort.

He'd been wild. This would have been his scene, but he was a Christian now. Was his whole sordid past flashing before his eyes? Everything he'd wished he'd never done. Her heart wanted to reach out and soothe him. Mustering up some courage of her own, she slipped her fingers through his. He bristled and glanced at their intertwined hands and then at her, questions in his eyes.

She gave him her most supportive smile. His past was

behind him. He was here for good. And she was standing with him. For him.

He cocked his head, studied her face and gave a small nod of acknowledgment, then he led her through the throng of people. Caley studied him as he observed the place. The people. If she didn't know why they were here, she wouldn't realize he was on a mission. Surveying. The man was good. He paused near the bar.

"I don't see anything," Caley said, her hand still in his. "Do you?"

He ignored her, watching the bartenders. No—one particular bartender. Caley watched. He didn't seem to be doing anything but delivering drinks to customers. What did Shep see that she didn't?

She gave up and spotted Ashley and Billy through the crowd. She squeezed Shep's hand and he nodded. "I see them."

Of course he had.

"We'll watch for now. See if they lead us anywhere. If not, we'll approach them."

Good plan. Shep continued to eye the bartender and a few patrons who wandered through the throng of people toward the back of the club.

A slow song played. "Let's dance, Little Flynn. You go to clubs to drink and dance. Since we don't drink…" He led her to the dance floor. Pulled her close, but not inappropriately so like some of the couples.

"I'm not a great dancer, Shepherd."

He peered down at her and grinned. "All you have to do is move with me, Little Flynn." He placed her hands around his neck. His warm hands slid down her back. "Just move with me."

Her stomach fluttered as she leaned into his chest and fell into step with him. Listening to a song about never saying goodbye.

At some point, she would say goodbye to Shepherd.

He would go back to Atlanta. Back to dangerous work.

And she would hopefully still have her job. Life would go back to being safe. Quiet. Normal.

She'd be alone again. That had never bothered her before. But now she realized how lonely it would be. How lonely she had been.

When the ballad came to an end, a faster beat picked up and Shepherd guided her off the dance floor. "Let's go talk to your interns," he said.

Caley approached them with a smile.

Ashley gaped. "Caley?"

"Hey."

Ashley glanced at Shep, letting her gaze linger a little longer than necessary.

Billy strode up with two drinks in his hand. "I can't find—" He froze, then grinned. "Caley? What are *you* doing here?"

Good question. She never went to places like this.

"I forced her to come. I heard this place is known for some serious bass," Shep offered, coming to her rescue.

"Totally," Ashley said. "If you can't feel it in your chest, it ain't strong enough."

Shep landed a killer smile on her. Ashley blushed.

Billy craned his neck up at Shepherd. "So you and Caley are…?"

"Together. Yeah." Shep slung his arm around her, drawing her to his side. "I travel for work."

Billy slid a glance her way. Was he buying it? "Well, we just came to blow off some steam."

"I was missing Mary Beth," Ashley said.

"Me too," Billy added.

Caley wasn't sure what to think. They didn't seem to be grieving. "Did she ever come here to blow off steam?"

"Mary Beth?" Billy chuckled. "No way. But she never

minded that I came." He heaped on a little more empha-
sis than necessary.

But they had proof she'd at least been to the club, if not
inside. Did Billy know that? Was he lying? Could there
be more going on between Ashley and Billy? If so, Mary
Beth might have suspected he was cheating and followed
him to the club to catch them. But catching her boyfriend
cheating with another intern, her friend, wasn't motive
to murder her.

"That was nice of her. Not to mind you hanging out
here." A shock of hair caught Caley's attention from the
back of the club. Was that Toby? "Ya'll have fun." She
needed to catch him before he left the scene. She left
Shep's arms and slipped through the crowd, but by the
time she made it to the restrooms, the exit door was closing and Shep grabbed her arm.

"What was that all about?"

"I think I saw Toby. From the lab." If it had been Toby.
She'd only caught the hair and a blip of a side profile.

Shep frowned. "You sure?"

"I know. I find it hard to believe he was here too, but I
thought... I don't know. We're not making any headway.
This has been a bust."

Shep's gaze landed on a scantily dressed woman. "I
wouldn't say that just yet."

A shot of hot jealousy burned through Caley. "She
pretty?"

He frowned. "I'm not looking at her. I'm looking at
her drink."

The woman carried a martini glass with a violet-colored
drink and a green umbrella poking out. "Why? What's so
special about her drink?"

Shep trailed the woman as she pushed through the
crowd to a back room. The shiny-headed brute who'd let
Leo in the back door stood guard. "Maybe nothing. But

I've seen at least five people order the same drink and from the same bartender." He pointed to the dark-haired guy flirting with a redhead at the bar.

"And why is that something?"

"It's called the Purple Turtle and it seems to be what gets them access to the back room that dude is guarding. No one else has been back there. The drink is the password so to speak."

Caley reeled. "No wonder my brother loves you on his team. I never picked up on any of that. And I was watching too."

"Yeah, well, you have to be extra observant when you've lived like I have."

If they weren't in a noisy club, Caley would ask him to expound. That was the longest sentence about his private life he'd given her so far and it was as she suspected. Oh, what Shepherd must have gone through as a child. Her heart ached for him.

"So what do you think is going on behind the door? You think they're buying turtles?"

Shep smirked. "No. But they all look like they're geared up for a seriously good time, if you get my drift." He studied the door, the burly guy standing in front of it. "The drink could be spiked with ecstasy, it's a major club drug…or they're buying it, or other drugs, back there. I'm not sure. But the drink's name interests me. Purple Turtle."

Caley spotted a guy with a purple drink. "Hey, he's got one. I could butter up to him and see if I could go back there with him."

Shep raised his eyebrows. "Not in a million years would I let you do that. And his umbrella is pink. You have to have the green umbrella to get in the back room."

Caley gaped. "I'm gonna call you Shepherd Holmes, Mr. Observant. All you need is the hat and pipe."

Shep laughed. "Let's keep you safe. I'll see if I can't go order the drink and get back there myself. Stay on this wall. Don't move."

"What about Toby?"

"If you did see him, he's long gone now."

"Okay. Go get the drink." She grabbed his arm as he made for the bar. "But be careful. These people are dangerous."

He smirked. "I can take care of myself." He paused. "And you."

Those words slid into her, turning her insides to warm bread pudding. Mmm…bread pudding. She should have eaten dinner. She frowned and edged to the back wall by the restrooms. The side exit door opened and several girls left giggling. The music blasted at deafening levels. Black lights replaced the neon lights, darkening the building, making it harder to see Shep's face but easier to see his white shirt. He leaned against the bar, making small talk with a girl while the bartender busied himself with customers.

Eerie shapes and patterns flashed across the walls. The bass thumped in her throat.

A cold chill crawled up her arms.

A strong arm hooked around her neck, locking her head in place so she couldn't turn.

*Shep!*

Grabbing the arm, she yanked, but it was strong and the attacker's grip tightened. Her purse that had been dangling in the crease of her arm was ripped from her, sending a sharp pain through her upper arm. She shrieked.

No one heard.

No one saw.

Bodies danced.

Voices cheered and laughed.

Shep leaned against the bar talking to the bartender who had been giving out Purple Turtle drinks.

The attacker thrust her forward and she bumped into someone, tripping and landing on her knees. More excruciating pain. Someone stepped on her fingers.

She turned to catch a glimpse of the man who'd strangled her and stolen her purse, but he was long gone in a sea of people, the exit door swinging shut. She sprang to her feet, her fingers throbbing, pushed through the crowd and poked her head outside.

No guy with her purse.

Just a few people milling about, smoking. Talking.

A hand grabbed her shoulder and she shrieked.

Shepherd. A mix of concern and a heated temper in his eyes.

He visually inspected her. "What happened? One minute you were right there and then you were gone."

"Someone stole my purse!" She gave him the rundown.

Shep balled his fist and pursed his lips. "I shouldn't have ordered that stupid drink."

"Where is it?"

"Forget the drink, Caley. Someone choked you and stole your purse. And I doubt it was a random snatch-and-grab."

Caley didn't believe it had been either. But now they had her purse and all her information. Not that they didn't know where she lived, but they had her driver's license. Her debit card. Her keys to everything important.

He gently tilted her chin up and to the right. "You're bruised already."

"I'm okay." She swallowed and put on a brave front. Shep had enough guilt on his shoulders and Caley didn't want him to think he'd failed to keep her safe.

"Any other injuries?" he asked.

"Just my fingers. They got stepped on, but I'm fine. Really." She ran a hand through her hair and inhaled deeply, hoping the jitters would settle soon.

"I shouldn't have left you."

"You had to get that drink." She pinched the bridge of her nose. "What happened?"

"I think he didn't trust me. I got turned down. Said they were all out for the night."

Lies. Shepherd had set off warning bells with the bartender. Too menacing-looking? "We've done all we can. Let's get out of here."

They strode across the street and Shep froze.

"What?" She turned her attention toward the parking lot.

Her car window had been busted, glass littering the inside of her car and the asphalt around the driver's-side door.

She gasped. "You have got to be kidding me!"

"Looks like he checked your car first and when that was a bust, he came inside. Got bold. He might think you're carrying what he's after in your purse."

"Well, I'm not!" Anger coupled with her fear. "The one time we didn't take the rental car." She threw her head back and groaned. "We've got to find this guy, Shep. He's turning my life upside down."

"I need to call Wilder."

No, what he needed to do was wrap her up in his arms and reassure her that this was going to end soon, without her having to ask for the physical contact. But he wouldn't. She closed her burning eyes. She'd just have to ask. Again. "Shep. I need more physical contact."

He licked his lips, hesitated only a second and then he drew her into his arms. Not like the first time. Not like on the dance floor. Like she belonged. Fit. No awkwardness. No pretending.

And here in his arms, safety abounded. Hope bloomed

that everything would be okay. Here she was sheltered in utter security. And it's where she wanted to stay the rest of the night.

Except a killer was coming for her.

# SEVEN

Shep stood behind the sliding glass doors, watching Caley sit on her patio with a cup of hot tea. How much more of this could she take? She was strong but everyone had a breaking point. He tapped Wilder's name on his phone and waited for it to ring, dreading the conversation to come.

Wilder picked up on the fourth ring. "It's late." His tone said it all. *Why was he calling? Why had Shep failed?*

"We had a run-in tonight, but Caley's safe." He briefed Wilder on the club action and how things went down and that Caley had insisted on going. "She's braver than you give her credit for."

Silence.

"She's holding her own." For now. "She's a Flynn through and through."

More silence.

What else could he say? "I'm sorry, bro."

"She's been hurt more than once. What if he'd kidnapped her from the club?" Simmering accusation was about to boil over through his words.

Shep fisted his hand. "I had her locked in. Glanced away. Turned back and saw she was gone. I immediately went after her. He wouldn't have gotten her."

"But he disappeared. Again."

"Roger that."

Wilder heaved a breath over the line. "Sounds like you're distracted."

"By what?" Anger bubbled up on his tongue. "This ain't vacation."

"Don't play dumb, Shepherd. Get your head in the game."

Wilder was too smart for Shep's vague attempt to act ignorant. "I am not distracted by the asset." By Caley. See, he could talk about her as a mission.

"She is not an asset. She's my baby sister and I expect you to keep her safe. I don't want another single scratch on her."

Neither did Shep. *"Roger. That."* He ground his teeth. He was distracted by the very person he was there to protect and it was going to get them both in trouble.

No more. He'd get his head back in the game like Wilder said. He was right anyway.

From the moment Caley walked into the kitchen, looking and smelling like a delicious dessert, to the way she melded against him on the dance floor, his brain had turned to mush and his heart had been palpitating. And to top it off she'd seemed to read his misery. Being in that club. All the mess going on there. That had been his past and he'd felt total shame, but she had taken his hand, and it chased that shame away. The compassion in her Irish-blue eyes, the encouragement in her sunshiny smile.

He couldn't put words to the way his heart took off on a roller-coaster ride, the way his blood heated and how much he desired to protect her. He'd never felt this way before.

And he couldn't explore what these feelings might be. He had a job to do.

"Call Tom. See if he has any idea what this Purple Turtle drink might indicate. Remember that six months we did in Bangkok?" Wilder asked.

Did he ever. Wilder had kept him from making some serious mistakes. Seen him at his wildest. But he wasn't that man anymore. He would never be that man again. Is that why Wilder kept at him about Caley… Wait… It dawned on him where Wilder was going with the conversation. They'd sold turtle eggs at the clubs, mixed them with ecstasy and slurped them down like oysters. They were considered an aphrodisiac. And they went for a pretty penny.

"Leo Fines might be poaching eggs."

His irritation tempered. "They might be selling them in the back room."

"I'll ask Tom about that too." Poaching sea turtle eggs was illegal. But it would be easy for someone like Leo to get his hands on them. Sell them for a nice profit. "Have you looked into Leo Fines's financials?"

"No, but I'll get Wheezer on it. Otherwise what we've found on Leo Fines is clean. Not even a parking ticket."

"See if there have been any larger deposits made. If he's selling turtle eggs or turtles, there might be a record if we follow the money."

"Or if he's selling both. I'll make the call," Wilder said.

"He might be getting some of these interns to do his dirty work. Maybe Mary Beth. I haven't mentioned that to Caley yet. I hate to break her heart again. She's had solid faith in the doctor and these kids."

"I wish Caley had better judgment. She adores that man and he's obviously shady and in on some criminal activity. I just wish she'd come home. Get a job in Atlanta," he huffed.

"She's a grown woman and doing really well here. Made a good life. Bad stuff happens. Doesn't matter where you work or live. It's just life. We don't get to escape it."

Silence.

"Do your job. And need I remind you that sniffing around my sister in any way that's other than sisterly isn't in your job description, Shep? She's already been hurt enough."

So Wilder trusted him to protect Caley, but he didn't trust him with Caley's heart. Didn't want to bring him into the fold of the Flynn family except from the outside where he'd always been anyway. Why would he? All he'd seen were Shep's mess ups. And Shep wasn't sure he wouldn't hurt Caley. He didn't have a clue about love, commitment. But the more he was near her, the more he wanted to know, to learn, to maybe…maybe try.

"I'm not going to make any moves on your sister." He didn't want to make moves. He wanted… He wasn't sure what he wanted. He was confused and frustrated. And scared out of his gourd.

"When I have news, I'll call you." The line went dead.

Shep had overstepped. But Caley had the right to be an independent woman without Wilder ordering her around or judging her choices. She'd made honorable ones. But Shepherd cut Wilder a break. He'd already lost one sister. Hovering over Caley was instinct, brotherly love and devotion.

Shepherd couldn't fault him, and he was well acquainted with Wilder's intense devotion to the people and things he was passionate about. He slid the glass door open and stepped out on the patio, taking a matching green Adirondack chair next to Caley.

Wrapped in a quilt, only her head and hands poking out, she reminded him of the turtles she loved so much.

"Breeze is a bit nippy," she said, and she sipped her tea.

The full moon cast a soft glow across her face. The *whoosh* of the waves relaxed his tense muscles; the taste of salt from the ocean dusted his lips.

He stretched out his legs. "Feels good to me."

Caley stared out at the dark waters. It wasn't hard to see why she loved living here. Soothing. Peaceful. If someone wasn't trying to kill her.

"My brother mad?"

"Yep." He locked his hands together on the back of his neck and looked up at the stars. The moonlight.

"You're a man of many words. You make me dizzy with all of them." She snickered and sipped the tea, a plume of steam rising, the smell of something flowery reaching him. He'd never been a talker. Never had much to say. And to be honest, he'd been ordered to stay quiet.

His voice or opinion had never mattered.

Glancing at Caley, her eyes held something he'd never seen before. Genuine interest.

"What do you want to know?" What if she asked a tough question? What if he scared her with his answers? Why did he even offer the chance for her to get a glimpse of him?

The answer scratched at the surface of his heart. He refused to itch.

Caley lowered her mug from her lips. "When did you place your faith in God?"

Not a tough question.

"In Afghanistan. Chaplain kept at me. Not in a fire-breathing-down-my-throat kind of way. Just…friendly-like. Casual conversation." He pawed his face. "After a mission went belly-up and several of my buddies died, I went through a dark time. Kinda like I was out in deep waters and unable to get to shore. Drowning."

Caley stopped sipping her tea, remained quiet. But she was listening. Urging him with a look to keep going.

"I remembered Chap saying Jesus was a lifeline. And I needed one. Had needed one for a long time, I guess. So

I prayed for the first time in my life and let Jesus rescue my soul from the depths."

"I'm glad to hear that, Shepherd."

"Chap gave me a Bible. And I stayed away from anything that resembled my old ways. I've done things I'm not proud of. I can't pretend I never did them." He pitched forward, elbows resting on his knees, his hands on his forehead. But he wished desperately that he could. Wished he had a clean past, could be good enough for someone like Caley.

Caley set the teacup on the table in between them and scooted her chair close enough to take his hands. "Shepherd, we all have things in our life we aren't proud of."

"Even you?" He doubted that Caley had ever done anything regrettable.

"Of course. I'm not proud for running away after Meghan died. My family grieved and they needed me to grieve with them, and I took a job here."

"But you love this job. This place."

"I do. But I don't love the way I left. I disappointed my family. Especially Wilder."

Shepherd stared at Caley's delicate fingers wrapped around his. "Wilder cares about you."

Caley nodded. "You can't let your past hold you back. You know that, right?"

She had a happy childhood. Didn't have a track record for making mistakes like he did. How many times could one person mess up before God called it quits? Sent him back into foster care?

"I know it shouldn't." But it did. "And I'm working to get it right more often. To be good."

Caley frowned. "Shepherd Lightman, you're a good man. Where is this coming from?"

He shrugged but didn't pull his hands away from hers. The way she held them made him feel safe. Secure.

This conversation was killing him. His heart beat uncontrollably, ached.

"Shepherd. Talk to me," she whispered.

He licked his lips. Took a deep breath. "When I did everything right. Kept my mouth shut and my head down... When I was good, I got to stick around longer with a family—hope for adoption. The minute I messed up I got sent back into the system. And one day I just decided it wasn't worth it anymore. So I stopped trying to be good. And I became really, really bad."

Tears welled in Caley's eyes. Why would she cry for him? "Shepherd." That one word. The way she said his name. More emotion behind it than he'd ever heard from anyone. He tightened his grip on her hands and choked back the lump growing in his throat.

Caley moved even closer, her knees brushing his. She ran her hand through his hair and rested it on his cheek. His walls crumbled faster than he could rebuild them.

The way she looked at him shifted everything inside.

The way she touched him. Like he belonged to her. He'd never belonged to anyone.

His gaze locked on hers. He couldn't tear it away, but then her eyes darkened and he recognized her intent. A shot of panic jolted him.

Shepherd couldn't give Caley what she deserved. And he hadn't intended for his words to make her feel sorry for him, pity him. He didn't want a pity kiss. If that was what was fueling her. And if it wasn't, well, as much as he wanted to feel her lips against his, it would mean something special to Caley. Something intimate that would require a commitment to come.

It slayed him, but he couldn't give her that. Wouldn't risk her heart. Couldn't risk his.

As she inched toward him, he slowly shook his head. "I'm not the guy for you, Caley. Don't go there," he whispered.

She paused, blinked away the hurt; her bottom lip trembled.

Hurt he'd evoked. Like he'd known he would at some point.

Proof he wasn't worthy of this incredible woman.

Wilder had been right. She'd been hurt enough, and now Shep could add his name to the list.

Caley slid back into her chair, tugged the quilt tighter against her.

Shepherd felt the chill in his bones too.

She closed her eyes. "You don't have to stay out here, Shepherd," she murmured, a hiccup in her voice.

"Gonna anyway." He may not be able to offer his heart. But he could offer his protection and he'd keep vigil, make sure she was safe.

Someone knew where she lived.

Someone who wasn't done yet.


Caley's eyes opened. She'd dozed off after Shepherd had rejected her.

He was right. He wasn't the guy for her. She had almost kissed the very man she'd promised herself she'd never fall for.

Blinking back the hurt, she stared at the moon. Round. Glorious. Romantic.

Waves crashed along the shore. They never failed to lull her to sleep, but the crick in her neck revealed she'd been in the patio chair awhile. Next to her, Shep dozed. His breath came soft and rhythmically. Like the waves.

What had she been thinking going in to kiss him? She

wasn't that bold. His raw honesty had moved her, touched her in deep places. He was tough. Intelligent. Rock solid. And vulnerable, tender and unsure of himself. That insecure little boy who desperately wanted to be loved still resided inside him. And for an instant, Caley had wanted to reach in and pull that little boy out, hug him, and also she wanted to kiss the man that boy had grown into. To kiss away his fear, to connect on an intimate level. To offer him…what? What could she offer him?

Love?

She didn't have that to give. Not to a soldier. Not to a man in his line of work.

She slipped from the quilt, the cup of tea long gone cold. Standing over Shep she studied his scar. Was it from war? Childhood? Who had hurt him? A need to protect him stirred within her. Even after he'd wounded her with his words. Truthful words. She respected that he'd stopped her. Thankful in a sense, because if she kissed Shepherd Lightman, she wasn't sure she'd be able to let him go. She was afraid her heart would slip over the edge, never to be found again.

But she'd ached to comfort him. Help him heal.

And he didn't want her.

Danger ran in his blood. A jarhead through and through. He'd never give that up for her. Never move here to the quiet beach life. And she would never ask him to.

So that was that.

Emptiness hit her full force.

She needed the cool waters on her feet. Needed to clear the fog from her head. Toes sinking into the sand, she padded toward the sea.

*God, show Shepherd how much You love him. How much You care. As far as the ocean is wide. And show me too.*

She squatted and held her hand out as the tide came in,

rushing over her fingers before it was pulled away. That's what would happen if she let herself love Shepherd. Collapsing in the wet sand, Caley drew up her knees and locked her arms around them. Sand and sea blanketing her, then leaving her cold.

She'd lost too many people she'd loved. To violence. When she left Atlanta, she believed she was running away from all forms of danger. Tucking herself inside a shell, like her turtles. But danger had come, poking its hazardous stick at her. She couldn't run again. Couldn't run fast enough if she did want to.

A presence sent pricks along Caley's neck.

She whipped around.

A man cloaked in darkness lunged and cut her shriek off with his hands. "Where is it?" he snapped. He shoved her head into the tidewaters. Salty sea invaded her nose, burning. Sand scraped against her cheek.

*Where is what?*

Reaching for his arms to release herself, she struggled, but he plunged her under the water again. A mouthful of ocean raced down her throat, choking her. She coughed and sputtered as he brought her back up again. Her hair matted to her face, masking her eyes.

"Tell me where the GoPro is. I know you have it!"

GoPro.

*GoPro!*

Mary Beth used her underwater video camera all the time. At the park. Used it on dives. She must have some kind of footage or photos incriminating someone.

"I don't…have…it!" Her head submerged again.

She kicked and flopped like a fish, flailing in hopes of knocking him off balance, gaining some oxygen. Her lungs burned, the taste of salt gagging her. Adrenaline shot through her veins and she grabbed at his face.

Ski mask.

If she could pull it off…

"Don't. Lie. To me!"

A crack fired and her attacker wailed, grabbing his shoulder and giving Caley time to kick him into the water. He fell into the tide and she clawed her way to the shore, gulping in air between coughs.

Raising her head, she spied Shep flying toward her, gun glinting in the full moonlight.

The attacker leaped from the water and sprinted across the beach, clutching his shoulder.

Shep had clipped him.

Saved her.

*Thank You, God.*

Instead of giving chase to the attacker, he kept running toward her. For her. Sliding to his knees next to her, he tucked his gun in his waistband, grabbed her shoulders and raised her up, shoving a mass of hair from her face. "Caley. Talk to me. Are you hurt?"

She shook her head, the coughing keeping her from speaking.

"Can you stand?" She managed a weak nod and he helped her to her wobbly feet, continued to hold her up, inspecting her for wounds.

"I know what he wants," she croaked. "He's after Mary… Beth's…GoPro."

She'd just been thinking of big threatening sticks being poked at her. This one had been the biggest. Someone was willing to drown her in the depths of the ocean to get the GoPro. Goose bumps rose on her flesh. From terror. From the chilly wind.

She shivered.

Shep paused. "Now would be a good time for physical contact, right?"

Yes, but it hurt too much accepting it from Shepherd. It might make her cling to false hope. "I just need to get dry." She forced a smile, knowing it was far from confident. "Just want to get inside my house."

He searched her eyes, then frowned. "I understand."

Did he?

They quietly walked up the beach to the bungalow.

"Why did you go down to the beach without me?" he reprimanded, as they approached the patio.

Caley cleared her scratchy throat. "I needed to think some things through. The beach is my place. My safe place…or…it was. How did he know I was out there?"

Shep didn't answer. Didn't need to.

The house was being watched.

"I won't do it again. You have my word."

He grabbed the quilt off the chair. "Dry yourself off some so you won't drip."

Shep wrapped the quilt around her—water seeped into the material, but it added some warmth. Not the kind she wanted, though. Not the kind that came from Shepherd's arms.

"The new question is what did Mary Beth do with her GoPro and what's on it? Pictures? Video? Both?"

Shep's sharp features hardened. "That's what I plan to find out. The Purple Turtle drinks, the duffel bag Fines took to the club, that back room along with the photo of the club Mary Beth took—they're connected."

"I agree."

"Wilder and I were talking and we think it's a possibility they might be selling turtle eggs back there."

Caley shivered again. "Why? For what?"

"Turtle eggs are sometimes used as an aphrodisiac and laced with drugs. Like ecstasy or PCP. It's possible that's going on at the Nest."

"You think Mary Beth discovered that? How? She wouldn't be able to find egg discrepancies."

"Unless she checked a nest and all the eggs were missing."

That landed a punch to Caley's gut. "You think Leo is poaching and selling eggs?"

"Possibly. And Mary Beth has photos or footage. It would ruin his career."

It could also be the nail in the center's coffin. All the donors would pull out. No grants. The program would fall to pieces. Nora Simms would have Caley blackballed.

But she had no choice. The right thing to do was to find the GoPro and put these monsters in prison—even if the trail led to Leo. "We need to go back to the club and order that drink. And get it this time."

"We'll worry about that later. You need to get into dry clothes and go to bed."

"I can do it." She had to. For Mary Beth. For herself. For the turtles.

He frowned. "Do what?"

"Go back in. I can wear a wig or colored contacts. You can't. Even if you changed your hair or eyes…"

"I have this whopper that can't be hidden." He pointed to his scar. "Past leaves its mark."

"Past as in war? Military?"

Cupping his neck, he broke eye contact. "I wish it had been forged with honor. But I'm afraid it was nothing more than a stupid brawl in my younger days."

"The past might leave marks, Shepherd, but it doesn't define who you are now." She half smiled and her teeth chattered. They might not be able to have a relationship with each other, but that didn't mean Caley couldn't help Shepherd see that he could move past his scars.

He touched his split eyebrow. "You see the good in everything, Little Flynn. I admire that." He opened the sliding glass doors and motioned her inside. "I'll call Jody and see if she's done with her escort detail in Washington."

"Wilder sent Jody to Washington?" Wow. Wilder could be insensitive sometimes.

"She wasn't happy about it."

Probably afraid of who she might run into while there. The man who wrecked her career. And her heart. "We don't need to fly Jody all the way here to order a drink. Let me at least try."

"No. I promised to keep you safe and I'm failing." He shut the patio door, locked it and closed the drapes.

Why didn't he see that he was far from failing? She was alive because of Shep. "You saved me out there. If you hadn't shot at him... You put a bullet in him."

Shep touched his sidepiece. "I grazed his shoulder. That bullet's in the water somewhere." He switched off the living room lamp, signaling she was to go to bed. "I won't willingly put you in danger."

"You can be with me every step of the way." She clutched the quilt closer. "Shepherd, I can't keep waiting for them to attack me again. I have to do something. Please, let me."

He shook his head. "I won't be able to go back in. If they see me, they might sniff you out. We may have already been seen together. Can't risk it."

"Then find a way. It's our only lead and it's slim, but we have to. I have to. I have to, Shepherd."

He blew out a heavy breath and licked his bottom lip. "Your brother won't like it."

"My brother isn't here. You are."

"I don't like it either."

"If you don't help me, I'll go alone. I promise you I will." She couldn't stay in her shell. She had to come out and do something. It was risky, and it might end badly, but she was done hiding.

Shep glared but she didn't back down from it.

Finally, he raked a hand through his hair. "Fine, Little

Flynn. But you are to do everything I say, when I say it and exactly how I say to do it."

She grinned. "Roger that, solider."

# EIGHT

Now that it was down to the wire and go time, Caley wasn't nearly as confident as she'd been last Saturday night when she'd put her foot down about going undercover at the Nest. She'd woken on Sunday morning and gone to church accompanied by Shep and Miss Whittle—who didn't seem to have a single worry. Shepherd had tried to talk her out of going in undercover, but when he'd realized she was as stubborn as a mule, he'd agreed and made a call to Tom.

Tom confirmed that the club was known for peddling drugs and that there had been a few busts in recent years, but nothing about selling turtle eggs. That didn't mean they weren't, though. He was still poking around unofficially, but he hadn't been able to turn up anything more than what Shepherd and Caley had.

She stood in front of her mirror and adjusted the honey-blond wig she was using for a cover, frowning at her overdone makeup. But she had a part to play. She couldn't fail.

Marching out of her bedroom, she splayed her hands at her side and looked at Shep. "Well?"

"I like you better as a brunette."

She smirked. Shepherd had been quiet these past several days, but that wasn't out of character for him. After he'd rejected her, she understood his need to keep an even wider distance between them. But she wasn't going to approach him again. Maybe he needed to know that.

"Hey," she said as he laid a dark bag on the coffee table. "I want you to know that I'm sorry about last Saturday. Outside on the patio. It won't happen again."

Pausing, Shep glanced at her. "Okay."

*Okay?* Seriously?

No point pushing him to express anything more. "Okay," she mumbled.

He retrieved a small black button thingy from the bag. "If you have any doubts," Shep said, "now is the time to tell me. I don't like this to begin with, and if Wilder finds out, he's going to come unhinged."

"Then he won't find out." Caley shrugged off the nerves. She had plenty of doubts, but they had to find out what was going on in that back room. It might be the only solid lead to finding Mary Beth's killer and the man attacking her.

"You aren't ready for this." He pinned her with a scowl.

Well, she had to be. "I am. And with all this getup you're about to put on me, it'll be like you're right beside me."

"I can't go in. Can't be seen with you. What choice did I have? Come here."

She stepped closer. "This is an earwig. You'll be able to hear me."

She nodded. The feel of his hands in her hair, moving it aside to place the earwig in her ear, reminded her of the day they'd parked in the driveway, pretending to care about each other. He'd run his hands through her hair.

"How does it feel?"

His hand? Amazing. The earwig? "Tight."

"Good." He locked his gaze on her, let her hair fall back over her ear. "Ready for the mic," he said with a husky voice.

She bit her bottom lip and nodded again.

"I'm going to pin it to your scarf."

Caley had chosen a long fitted black T-shirt and a funky lightweight scarf as an accessory. Shep stepped even closer. He pinned the small microphone underneath her scarf. "You'll be able to talk to me. But try not to. We don't want anyone catching you." He frowned. "I don't like not being able to be in there physically."

"It's going to be fine." She'd been telling herself that for hours. "Let's go."

They climbed in Shepherd's rental car and made their way to the Nest. Shep dug into the bag again and pulled out a purse. "Camera built in."

"How did you get all this?"

"Favor from Tom."

"I'm surprised you didn't have him put an undercover officer on this." She snorted, but Shepherd didn't laugh.

"I tried. But since they aren't investigating officially, he couldn't. And he's done some busts in there, so they'd recognize him."

"Oh." She chewed on her bottom lip. "Okay. I'm going to order the drink and pray that it works and gets me into the back room to see what's going on. Hopefully, if you're right about the turtle eggs, I'll spot some and get it on camera." She placed the purse's strap on her shoulder.

"You may get proof that they're selling illegal turtle eggs and drugs without getting proof that anyone at the center is connected. Maybe we'll catch a break and Leo Fines or one of your interns will be in there and we can get them dead to rights."

That was a souring thought. More than ever they needed to find Mary Beth's GoPro. She had some kind of proof or she wouldn't have ended up dead. They'd called Mrs. Whaling and inquired about it, but she said they hadn't found it even though they'd specifically hunted for it. They wanted to see all the things Mary Beth had seen. Caley was pretty sure they didn't. Something she'd seen had gotten her killed.

They'd searched everywhere. It was like it had disappeared, just like her phone. Wheezer hadn't been able to locate it. Shep thought it was probably in the ocean, corrupted by the salt water. The GoPro wouldn't be, though. Mary Beth might have hidden it. But why? Why hadn't she come to Caley?

Frustration knotted her muscles.

"It's Thursday Ladies' Night. Go in and go straight to the bar. Flirt a little with the bartender, then order the Purple Turtle." Shep expelled a breath and adjusted his earwig. "I'll drop you at the end of Tourist Row and you can walk from there. If you get into trouble and need me just say, 'Is it me or is it hot in here?' and I'll come for you."

Caley felt like she'd swallowed a jar of jumping beans. Her hands turned clammy. *God, help me do this.* "Got it. Is it me or is it hot in here?"

Shep drove his rental to the end of the Tourist Row. It was after nine. The sun had dipped and the clubs were in full swing. She gripped the side of the passenger door when Shep edged near the curb.

"You're brave, Caley. You can do it. I don't like it but not because I don't think you can handle it. I just don't want anything to go sideways."

Not helping.

"See you on the flip side." She opened the car door and ambled down the sidewalk in between people milling about or sitting at outdoor tables enjoying the summer night with friends. She neared the Nest.

*God, help me.*

Showtime.

Inside cigarette smoke and deafening music blasted her senses, but she pasted on a smile that hopefully let people know she was here for a good time. Women had packed the place. She squeezed through them, whispered without minimal mouth movement, "I'm heading to the bar."

"I see it." Shep's voice filled her ears. "Don't talk to me unless you have to, and don't fidget with your scarf."

"Where are you?"

"I'm in the alley behind the Dumpsters. And what did I just say?"

Nerves. Okay, she was shutting up now, but knowing he was nearby helped. She waited until a bar stool opened and slithered onto it, catching the eye of the bartender from the other night. Nice-looking. Dark hair. Scruff. A little John Stamos-ish. He made his way to her, a flirty grin meeting her first. He leaned on the bar, close to her.

"Give me a break," Shep muttered.

Caley ignored him.

"Now, I'd know if I'd seen you before," the bartender said. He pointed to himself. "Rob."

"Meghan." First name that popped into her head. "My friends call me Meg." Her sister had never liked being called that.

Dimples creased his cheeks. "What about me? Can I be a friend?"

"You can call me Meg." She winked and tried not to vomit. This guy was a total letch.

"You come alone?" he asked.

Oh boy. Where was this going? "I did, but…I'm hoping I don't stay that way."

His laugh oozed down her spine like slime, but she had to play the part. How did undercover cops and agents do this day in and day out?

"You're flirting too well, Little Flynn, which begs the question…how do you know how to flirt that well?" Shep's grit and gravel traveled straight to her middle. She loved that voice.

"I don't see you staying alone for long, Meg. What can I get ya?" Rob asked.

"For now?" she cooed, leaning close to him, close enough to smell expensive cologne. "Just a Purple Turtle," she whispered, hoping it sounded seductive and finishing it off with a wink and a suggestive smile.

"You are waaaaay too good at this, Flynn," Shep groused.

But no *Little*. That sent a thrill through her. She shoved it aside, focused on the task.

Rob raised his eyebrows. "A Purple Turtle. Well now. And how would you know about those drinks?"

"I know a lot of things I shouldn't." She held his gaze. Her stomach was a rage of nerves, the back of her neck breaking out in a sweat.

Shep coughed, cleared his throat, then she heard the sound of a fist beating against his chest as if he had something lodged there.

Too many beats passed as Rob sized her up. Was she busted?

Finally, he grinned. "I'm sure you do. I'm here till close. I'll come find you after."

"Do that, Rob." She'd be long gone. He grabbed a few bottles and mixed the drink, then shook it before pouring it into a martini glass and adding a green umbrella. He sat it in front of her.

"On the house, Meg. Since we're friends, and hopefully better friends later." He winked again.

She raised her glass and slid of the stool. "BFFs. See you at closing."

"You definitely will."

Without spilling the drink, which she had no intention of drinking, she slipped through the crowd. "I did it. I can't believe it."

"I can't believe you didn't walk out with the drink and

his bank account number and password. Way to work it, woman."

"Don't tell my brother!" she begged.

He chuckled.

"I'm heading to the back room door. That same bouncer is there again. What do I do?" she whispered.

"Be cool. Hand him the umbrella. That's what they did Saturday night. Raise your glass but say nothing."

"Then what?"

"Let's take it one step at a time."

She followed his order and the door was opened to a large back room. Decorated just like the front but on a smaller scale. Some of the things she saw going on... She wanted to bolt. But a guard stood at the door on this side too. "Do you see this?" she whispered again.

"Yeah. And I don't like it. At all. Set your drink down at that bar and excuse yourself to the bathroom. Get out of there."

"I have to see if I can get us some proof. Of something."

"Caley," Shep warned. "You said you'd do what I told you to and when I told you to. I'm telling you to abort the mission. These people are drunk, high and looking for the kind of time you aren't willing to give."

"Five minutes."

He growled over the mic.

She made her way to the bar, bobbing her head to the electronic beat. Trying to fake being comfortable. That's when she spotted a tray and two bouncers guarding it. She shifted on her stool, for the camera to pick up.

"I see it, Caley. Now abort."

A tray full of turtle eggs cracked open like oysters. People paying their money and slurping them down.

Her stomach roiled.

She set her drink on the bar. Time to go. A blond guy approached her with an egg. "Hey, gorgeous. Shall we?"

"Tell him yes, but you need to hit the bathroom first," Shep said, his tone stern. Forceful.

"Oh, we shall. But I need to go to the ladies' room. Wait for me?" She smiled.

"I'll be right here."

She checked out her surroundings. Debauchery in full swing. And she'd be required to participate if she hung around. Fear raced through her blood. The burly guy at the door frowned as she approached him. He'd seen her just come in. People in here planned to stay awhile. "I need to go out and use the restroom."

"Bathroom's up there." He pointed to a wrought iron staircase leading upstairs.

"Oh, it's my first time." She laughed, but heard the anxiety in it.

Shep piped up in her ear. "Relax. There has to be an exit somewhere on this side of the building. Go up to the bathroom. Pull it together."

"I can tell." The bouncer pointed upstairs again, but the way he looked at her gave her a major case of the willies.

Caley weaved through the partying. The guy waiting for her wasn't at the bar anymore. She climbed the stairs, breathing deep. Evenly. *You got this, Caley. Calm down. Think straight.* Upstairs a long hallway curved to the right. "Maybe I can find a way to get down a fire escape."

"Just go into the bathroom, Caley."

She inched down the hall. What were all these rooms? Horrible images flooded her brain and sent her sprinting, but a familiar voice coming from one of the rooms pricked her ear.

She paused and turned to the door.

"Go. To. The bathroom, Caley." His tone came with much more force.

Ignoring Shepherd, she cocked her ear to the door.

Leo.

"This is out of control," Leo said.

So her mentor had sold them eggs. Tossed his integrity out the door for greed.

"Caley," Shep barked.

A large hand clasped her shoulder with some serious grip. "This isn't the bathroom," the guard from the door boomed. "Come with me."

Oh no. No. No. She shook all over; her pulse thumped in her temples. "Where are we going?"

He turned her down the hall and to the left. Only two doors. He opened one of them and shoved her inside. "Sit down. I think the boss man might want to chat with you." Another goon stepped inside. Burly Guy pointed at him. "Stand outside the door. Make sure this little honey doesn't go anywhere."

"I was just looking for a bathroom," Caley said.

"Remain calm, Little Flynn. I'm with you. Not gonna let anything happen."

She exhaled, shakily. Turned around the room so Shepherd could see everything. A desk. A couple black leather chairs. A window facing the alley.

"I'm behind the Dumpster. I got eyes on you."

Eyes wouldn't save her.

Burly Guy grabbed her chin, jolting her. Shep growled through the mic. "Uh-huh. I've been watching you. You ain't here to party."

Caley held back a whimper.

"Sit tight. I'm coming for you," Shep said.

"But we're gonna find out why you are here, pretty thing."

She didn't need a code word. It was clear she was in serious trouble.

Shep hustled across the alley, keeping a calm head, but his heart hammered against his ribs. He wasn't sure who they thought Caley was. A reporter. Police. Didn't matter. Nothing good was going to happen and he didn't see them letting her go. Especially when they searched her and found the camera, mic and earwig.

But that bouncer wouldn't get the chance to lay another hand on her. Shepherd was sure he had by Caley's flinch. His blood boiled at the thought of someone inflicting pain on her.

He scanned the perimeter.

Caley was in the room, probably an office, above him. The same room where he'd seen the curtain shift that day they followed Leo.

She was in the room alone now. One guy getting "boss man" and the other guy outside her door. Two men were nothing. He could take them down with his eyes closed, but he didn't know how many more were inside, and Shep couldn't risk getting Caley hurt.

"Shep," Caley whispered with a catch in her voice. "Are you still there?" Every single syllable held fear. He should have gone with his gut and refused her access to the club. But he understood her need to feel strong, to fight back.

"You don't see me because I don't want to be seen. Now quit talking. Sit down. There might be cameras in the office." She was in the room without the fire escape. Not good. A bouncer stood at the corner of the alleyway. The only way up was through him.

He stayed to the shadows and sneaked up behind the guard. One precise maneuver to the neck and the dude dropped. Out cold, but that would only last about three minutes. He raced up the fire escape and peeped into the window. Empty. But he couldn't be sure someone wasn't out in the hall.

Shep needed this to go down quiet and fast. Taking down only those he needed to. If he caused a commotion in the hallway leading to Caley, it could get her killed. If he caused a commotion coming out, he could shield her. Either way was going to be a risk.

He glanced at the window that opened to the office Caley was being held hostage in. The ledge protruding from it was narrow, not even a foot wide. But it was his only choice. He'd have to jump, and pray his foot made the ledge and he had enough grip on the brick to secure himself.

One deep breath and he lunged, his foot solidly landing as he gripped the window and tapped. "Caley, let me in."

Caley rushed to the window and opened it. He placed a finger on his lips, motioning her to be quiet, and jumped inside, then surveyed the room. The minute they busted through the door, it would incite a gun war. How many men were out there?

They didn't have much time. Any minute they'd bring up the "boss man."

Shep glanced up. Hatch to the roof. All these old buildings would have them. *Thank You, God.* If they could go up onto the roof, there should be another fire escape on the other side. They could climb down and call it a day.

He checked the window again and a black sedan pulled to a stop. A man with thick black hair and an expensive suit stepped out. Shep grabbed his phone, turned off the flash and took a photo, hoping it wouldn't be too dark to see later.

"Boss man is here." Manager. Owner. Shep wasn't sure, but he was the big enchilada with an entourage of men surrounding him. "We gotta go up, Little Flynn."

Caley was in danger however he played it, but he needed to move fast. Grabbing a chair, he climbed up and unlatched the hatch to the roof, thankful for the blaring music below masking the thud of it opening.

"Come on," he called.

"What will we do once we get up there?" Caley's voice was strained and she was hugging her forearms.

"I hope we can make it across the roof and down the fire escape before they realize we're gone. So put some fire under your boots and come on." He took her hand and she climbed onto the chair, hyperaware of their close proximity. "I'm gonna boost you up."

"Okay," she stammered.

"Ready?" He gripped her waist and lifted her into the air. She used her arms and hoisted herself up and out. Shep put the chair back in place and used his core and leg strength to jump, grabbing on and pulling himself up, then he closed the hatch. He ran across the roof, peering over the sides.

His lungs turned to iron.

No second fire escape.

It wouldn't take long for whoever came into the room to figure out they'd gone up. They couldn't go back down. He glared at the building on the other side of the alley. A gap just five feet across separated them from that structure. Not bad. Caley, at about five foot three, didn't have a long stride, though.

*God, help me out here.*

He faced her. Her skin had turned ghostly white. "Ever play hopscotch?"

"Why?" she asked, caution in her tone.

Shep motioned with a tilt of his head to the edge of the roof.

Caley's sight went straight to the other side of the roof and she rushed over, peering down into the alley that separated the buildings. Sweat popped on her forehead, mouth agape, head shaking furiously. "I can't do that. I can't jump across there. I'm not a soldier! I study turtles!"

"Slow and steady ain't gonna win this race."

"No! Just…pop 'em the minute they come up. You're

a sniper! You can do that." Her voice reached window-cracking volume and she flailed her hands wildly.

"Caley," he said, his voice low and calm while inside he was reeling. "I'm not going to do that." Not that it hadn't crossed his mind, but she might get caught in the cross-fire, and he wouldn't risk it. "And you don't really want me to." Caley would never condone killing no matter who it was. That wasn't who she was. But she was panicking. And if she didn't try her best to relax, she'd hesitate on the jump and plummet to the alley below.

Time was thin. Any minute they'd make it upstairs. Into the office. And that would be that.

"You're a Flynn. You can do it. I know you can do it. Trust me." Why should she, though? He'd put her in this predicament.

She licked her lips, wrung her hands together. Blew a breath. "I'm gonna be sick."

No time to patty-cake anymore. He hardened his tone. "You're gonna jump to that building and you're going to make it." He'd give her no choice. "I can't go first. You gotta go." He wasn't leaving her with criminals to show up and him not here to defend her.

She raised her hands to her blond wig and fisted two handfuls. "Okay. Okay, I'll do it." She nodded. "I can do it." Seemed she was more psyching herself up than convincing Shep, and panic laced her tone.

What would ease her? His words weren't doing the job. He'd been sweet about it. And rough.

Physical contact.

That's what made her feel safe.

He tugged her against him, gripped her in a firm embrace. "You got this, Flynn. And I'll be right behind you." She burrowed against him and a pent-up breath released. "You can do this. You're the bravest, strongest woman I've ever met." He pulled back to peer into her eyes, framed her face. "You run with all you got, spring off and push your body forward."

She nodded emphatically.

Fog cleared from her eyes. Courage rested in place of fear.

"Now."

She positioned herself into a runner's pose. "One, two, three..." She ran like the wind and hurled herself off the building.

Shepherd silently prayed, his stomach in knots and sweat slicking down his back.

Caley had it! She was going to make it.

She shrieked.

Shepherd's heart lurched into his throat.

Her foot landed on the edge of the other building's roof, but slipped.

She fell backward.

"Caley!"

Shepherd burst across the roof.

Caley grasped on to the ledge with one hand, dangling. "Shepherd," she cried, "I can't... I'm slipping!"

Shepherd landed on his feet, knelt.

Caley's fingers continued to slip.

Four left...

Three...

He grabbed just as the last finger slid away. With an iron grip on her wrist, he hauled her into his arms, not because she might need it, but *he* did. "I've got you. You're safe."

The roof door sprung open.

"Get them!" someone barked.

Shots fired.

# NINE

Caley squealed and ducked. Shepherd shielded her and shoved her forward. "Run for the roof hatch," he barked.

Shots continued to fire. Concrete sprayed in the air. Men yelled.

Caley couldn't hear. Couldn't process.

Her pulse roared in her ears and she couldn't catch her breath.

Shep grunted as he yanked the roof hatch open. "Down. Let's go."

Caley scrambled down the roof hatch and dropped into what looked like an office in this restaurant's second floor. Shep dropped behind her.

Chatter and the smells of Cajun spices hit her senses, but Shep didn't give her time to get her bearings before he yanked the blond wig from her head and tossed it, cracked the office door, scanned the hall, then dragged her beside him as he strode down the hall.

"They'll be waiting for us outside. They won't make trouble in the building but we can't stay in here all night."

Caley's breath was shaky and her hands trembled, her knees wobbled. She needed a minute to pull it together but she didn't have a minute. "I jumped off a roof." How had she done that?

"You did good."

"I could have died."

"But you didn't." Shepherd paused. The clatter of dishes, laughter and chatter grew closer. Must be an upstairs dining area, as well. He laced his hand in hers. "Smile," he whispered as they approached round tables with soft candlelight. Diners enjoying a meal. Oblivious to the fact that Caley and Shepherd were running for their lives.

Shep never stopped scanning, calculating. Caley thanked God for his set of unique skills.

A server stepped in front of them and Shep moved behind him, like a shield, following him down the stairs into the main dining area and to the swinging kitchen doors.

"What now?" Caley asked.

"We're going out the front doors and blending into the crowd. They won't shoot us in a crowd."

"But what if they're standing out there?"

"Count on it." Shep guided her past tables. Outside the glass windows, the streets were packed with people. "But it's our best shot. Keep your head down, lean into me." Shep shoved the front doors open. A mix of smoke, spices and perfumes hit Caley like a ton of bricks.

Her chest continued to pound, but she trusted Shepherd with her life. If anyone could get them out of here safely, it was him. She pressed into him and kept her head down as he bobbed in and out of the sea of people.

Two guys in front of them laughed and carried on a conversation about the local college football team. Shep tapped one guy's shoulder. "Hey, I'll give you a hundred bucks for your ball caps."

"You serious, dude?"

Shep scanned the throng of people, reached into his pocket and brought out two fifties.

"Sweet!"

The college-aged guys gave Shepherd the hats and pocketed the money. Shep slid a ball cap onto Caley and on himself.

"I can't believe you gave that guy a hundred dollars."

"I'd have given five hundred if I knew it would keep you safe, Little Flynn." He paused and someone bumped into them, cursed and moved around them.

"What is it?"

"Up ahead." Burly Guy and a lanky man. "Plan B." He zigzagged and cut into a comic-book store. A few graphic novel geeks looked up. A guy with thick black-framed glasses and unruly hair nodded.

"You looking for something in particular?"

"Your office," Shep said and the cashier's eyes went round like saucers. "This girl's ex-boyfriend tried to attack her. Him and his friends are casing the strip. We need a place to hide out until it's clear."

The cashier didn't seem to buy the story.

Caley stepped forward. "Please, help me. He'll kill me if he finds me. He's crazy." The desperation in her voice wasn't an act, her words never truer. "Please. You'd be a superhero." Maybe that would stroke his ego. He did work in a comic-book store.

He darted his sight from her to menacing Shepherd. "Okay. But just for a few minutes. I'm not supposed to let anyone back there."

Caley grabbed his hand. "Thank you."

His cheeks turned pink and he led them to the back office.

"If anyone comes in and asks if you've seen us, the answer is no." Shep gave him a stern look. "And remember, I can hear you from in here."

"Yes, sir."

The cashier went back out.

Shepherd hurried to the exit that led into the alley but

stayed indoors. "We have a better chance staying in the crowd, but…" Frustration laced his voice. "You holdin' up?"

Barely.

"I think so," she whispered.

He turned from the door, held her gaze.

"Thank you."

"It's my job." He looked away.

Was the physical contact, the embrace that had given her the comfort and strength she needed to brave the jump, been his job? Should she ask?

Now wasn't the time.

"I know I've already said it, but I can't believe I jumped off a roof." She bent at the knees, the aftershock stealing her breath.

"Wilder's going to kill me."

"Kill you? He should kiss you."

"Kiss me? I nearly got you killed. I broke my word— I promised to keep you safe. I keep saying I'm sorry. It's true."

"Shepherd Lightman!" A white-hot heat drove through her veins. "How can you say that? I'd be dead if it wasn't for you. Who knows what they'd have done to me before murdering me? All you've done is keep me safe. Rescue me. Risk life and limb for me. Stop saying you've failed or I'll… I'll… I don't know what I'll do!"

His Adam's apple bobbed as he swallowed.

While she was feeling brave, she might as well jump. She was getting good at it. "You hugged me." She strode across the office and straight into his personal space, causing him to shift. "Physical contact."

"I did." He had more grit and gravel in his voice.

"Was that just doing your job? Or…or was something behind it?" She had to know. Shepherd didn't give affection freely. But he'd given it to her. What was backing it up? Did he…did he care about her? Caley the person and not Caley the assignment?

Would it matter? She wanted to confidently believe it wouldn't. But she'd be lying. She cared for Shepherd more than she should. More than she wanted to. Confusion whirled in her heart.

He shrugged one shoulder. "Physical contact calms you down. You were so scared. Seemed the right solution." He refused to look her in the eye.

"Well, don't do it again." She held back burning tears. She was just a mission. It had been a means to an end. He probably didn't think she was brave or capable. Those were simply words to get her to jump. To do what he wanted. Soldiers accomplished their missions no matter what it cost. Right now it was costing her heart. "Am I clear, solider?"

He sighed and stepped forward, opened his mouth to speak but clamped it shut.

"Am. I. Clear?"

"Roger that," he muttered. "I'm going out front. Stay here."

"Roger that," she repeated. She needed a minute to pull it together. To win the war going on inside her. *You can't love a soldier, so stop pining for one. Stop it right now, Caley. He's not the guy for you. He said it himself.*

Shep came back inside the office. "We're movin' out."

She inhaled deeply. "On your six."

He nodded and they left the comic-book shop, Shepherd sticking to her like glue. They made it to the car. He opened the door for her and rounded the hood to his side. Inside, he cranked the engine. "I'm going to call Tom. Let him know what happened and get some information on the club's owner and manager. Get Wheezer on it too. He can pull off a few things Tom might not be able to."

Back to business. Fine.

Shep gave her a sidelong glance. "Put your seat belt on. Last thing I need is a car accident irrelevant to all this mess injuring you."

She clicked her belt into place with more force than necessary.

Silence remained until they reached her bungalow. Miss Whittle had already gone to bed. Caley switched a lamp on in the living room. She listened as he called Tom and then Wilder. She walked to the kitchen.

His neck was red and a vein popped out along the side. His fist rested on the counter. "I'm not interested in your sister, Wilder. Give me a break."

He'd made that clear, but hearing confirmation stung. Caley held back burning tears.

"She's fine," he said. "Shaken up, I expect… Okay. Seriously?" He groaned and spun around.

Busted.

He froze, cocked his head and licked his bottom lip, then jabbed the phone toward her. "He wants to talk to you."

She didn't want to talk to Wilder. She wanted to bury her head in her covers and not come out until this was over, but she couldn't. Caley took the phone. "Hello?"

"How are you? Honestly," Wilder said.

"A few scrapes and bruises but I'm in one piece." She glanced at Shep but he'd turned his back on her. In more than one way.

"You sure?"

She rolled her eyes. "I'm fine. Shep's kept me safe."

"You don't sound safe to me," Wilder boomed.

She snapped. "Well, how would you know? You're not here."

He sighed over the line, softened his tone. "I wish I were. I'm sorry. I just love you."

And she loved Wilder. But he was overprotective, and

what had he asked Shepherd that caused him to respond that he wasn't interested in Caley? Wilder might want her safe, but he had no business meddling into her private relationships. The buck stopped there. But with Shepherd standing next to her, she wasn't going to ask. "I love you too."

"Get some sleep."

She was going to try.

"Talk to you soon." She hung up and handed Shep back his phone. He messed with it for a minute. "Tom said a guy named Kyle Marx owns the Nest. Google had some images. It's the same guy I saw getting out of the car." His thumbs ran over the phone keyboard. "Texting Wheezer to get us info on him."

No way could she sleep. She ran her hand through her hair. "I'm going to make myself some tea. I don't think I can eat. But if you're hungry, I can make you a sandwich."

He tipped his head, squinted. "You...you wanna make me a sandwich?"

"Well, yeah." How hard was it to slap some ham and cheese between two pieces of bread?

"I thought you were mad at me."

"I am, sort of. Doesn't mean I'm going to withhold food from you. Do you want a sandwich or not? You haven't eaten."

If ever she'd seen a confused expression, this was it. "I... Yeah, okay." His voice sounded like an unsure little boy.

A sudden thought knocked her off balance. "Shepherd, did your foster parents do that to you? When they were mad?"

He stared at the floor.

Answer enough. She wanted to find the names of those evil people and...and...every violent thought ran through her mind. How could adults do that to a child? "Shepherd, I'm so sorry."

"Don't be. Helped me in the end…to be a better solider."

He could justify it all he wanted. It was *not* okay. The urge to wrap him in a hug hit her, but she'd just told him no more physical contact, and he'd probably shrug her off anyway. Instead, she made him the biggest ham-and-cheese sandwich and topped it with a pickle and chips. She brought it to the table and lightly touched his shoulder before putting a kettle of tea on for herself.

Shep scrolled through his phone while he ate, casting side glances her way every now and again.

"Mary Beth knew her attacker. Lack of defensive wounds. After tonight, I'm even more convinced it was Leo Fines. She trusted him."

"Why would she go swimming with Leo?" Caley asked. "Unless he's Mystery Man."

"Let's say he is. Why would she kayak and swim alone at night with him right out in front of the center and dormitory? Someone would see them. And interns have said she was being sneaky and going out late at night. That wouldn't be too sneaky, would it?"

"So the Mystery Man theory is probably moot." Caley wanted to scream. They still didn't have enough to put a *who* to the list.

"Based on what we heard and saw tonight, yes. I think she discovered the eggs were being poached and sold inside the club and went to Leo."

"So explain the swimsuit."

Shep finished off his sandwich and pushed his plate away. "I have no solid proof, but what if the swimsuit was placed on her after? She could have met Leo somewhere else with the information. Maybe even in his office late at night. Then she was placed in front of the center to make it look like an accident, and she drifted."

Caley sank farther in her chair, the tea not offering the relaxation it typically did. "And we can't approach him with this new theory."

"No. And we have the GoPro to find."

"If she was going to go to Leo, wouldn't she have taken it with her? To show him the footage? Or someone. We can't be sure it was Leo who killed her."

"True. But he's looking like the best suspect."

"He was talking to someone. He said it was getting out of control. He's not in this alone."

Shep wadded his napkin. "No. He could have been on the phone with Kyle Marx, the club's owner and manager."

"Maybe that's what he was doing up there. Waiting for Kyle to arrive."

Nodding, Shep stood, carried his plate to the kitchen and loaded it in the dishwasher. "I don't know where that GoPro is. Or what caused it to slip from the killer's grips, but it's the key to this."

"If she was killed elsewhere, maybe she dropped the GoPro or hid it to keep the killer from it." She chewed her nail. "But that doesn't make sense because she wasn't afraid of her killer. She had no defensive wounds. No skin or blood under her nails."

"She might have gone in trusting him, and gotten spooked. Hid the GoPro. Who knows? But Leo Fines, Kyle Marx and even that bartender are in on this. What was his name again?"

Heat flushed her cheeks. She'd forgotten about that display. "Rob."

"Rob." He folded his arms over his chest, but didn't press the issue about how she'd learned to flirt like he said he would. "And what about Ashley, Billy and Toby? They could all be in on this too. They can be tied to the club. They have access to the eggs and logbooks and Mary Beth trusted them."

She ran her finger along the edge of her mug. "But the intruder at the dorm room, the club that night, on the beach. That wasn't Leo. Maybe he could mask his voice, but not his physique. He's at least a foot taller than whoever attacked me and more slender with a runner's build. Not beefy."

"Could be any one of those cronies at the club."

"True. But why do they think we have the GoPro if she took it with her to show evidence or to confront them? She must not have taken it at all."

"Or something else, Caley. Something you don't want to believe. But Mary Beth might have been in on this and was blackmailing someone, and it got her killed. Now the killer is on the hunt for the footage to make sure no one else finds out."

Caley couldn't swallow that pill. But then she'd never dreamed Leo was crooked. "My head hurts." She rubbed her temples. The GoPro was the key. She jumped up. "We can track it! They make devices to track GoPros. It's easy to lose them because they're used in rugged terrain, underwater, at high speeds. If she had one, she would've placed the device on the body of the GoPro to connect it to an app. The app on her phone would allow her to keep tabs on it at all times. And the app will be in her iCloud account." Excitement bubbled.

Shep smiled. "You ever think about getting a job with Crisis Covenant Management? You'd make a good detective."

Not in a million years. Especially after all the danger they'd been through tonight. "I don't even want to watch crime shows anymore. I don't know how you do it."

"Somebody's got to. And I like helping people who are in trouble get free." He picked up his cell phone. "I'm going to call Wheezer. Check to see if she has that app that links to the GoPro and if she does, he can track it once he gets the password. Might take a couple days or he could pull it off in minutes. Who knows with him? Go on and get some shut-eye. If I have something before morning, I'll wake you."

She almost refused, but she was exhausted, and what more could she do but stew and pace the floor? Although, she doubted she'd sleep. They were closer than ever to discovering the truth.

Shep sat in one of the Adirondack chairs on Caley's patio, watching the sun rise until he could wake Caley. The past few days had consisted of Caley going about her typical routine, trailing Leo, which got them nowhere, and checking in with Tom at TBPD and Wheezer.

Mary Beth had the app and tracking device, but Wheezer was having more trouble cracking the password than he had with her Apple password. Mary Beth's parents had tried to help by searching for a password book, but it was a dead end.

Until this morning when Wheezer had called right after Shep had made a new pot of coffee at 0300 hours. He'd cracked the password. But Shep wanted Caley to get some sleep. They could go after the GoPro when the sun rose.

She'd been through the trenches the past couple of weeks. All the attacks on her. The night at the club had almost done her in. Almost done him in too. Emotionally. He hadn't lied to Caley. He did know she used physical contact for comfort. What he didn't say was that drawing her to him, even for a moment, had felt oddly right. Like the closest thing he'd ever had to home. He couldn't, wouldn't, share that truth. And her comments about not wanting any part of the kind of life Shep lived only confirmed he wasn't the guy for her.

But she didn't understand what it was like to constantly feel trapped and want help getting out of a bad situation. She didn't know the frustration and fear of being bounced from one family to another and none of them being good ones. They were out there. But Shepherd had never once landed on their doorstep.

Freedom meant everything to him. Helping others find it meant equally as much. It was tough and dangerous, but it also came with satisfaction. And he hoped it made up for all the mistakes he'd made. That God would see the good he was doing now and not leave him. Not change his mind about Shepherd.

Because Shep made mistakes often. He'd hurt Caley. Made her mad. Frustrated her.

And she'd offered to make him a sandwich. She'd shown him grace he certainly didn't deserve. It baffled him. She was so unlike the women in his childhood, who'd withheld love from him often. In the form of food. Physical contact. Verbal affirmation. He'd gotten used to it. Tried to do better and, when he'd failed, given up.

Channeled all that pain into being an unemotional soldier.

Until Caley Flynn.

How could one woman be so incredibly soft and tough as steel all at once? She was the bravest woman he'd ever met. She was kind and good and everything he'd always wanted to be. She'd pulled his past from him, and while it was bitter, it had also been freeing. The woman didn't judge. Didn't call him stupid—like so many before. If he had any idea how to love a woman, she'd be the exact person he'd want to make a go of it with. Longer than a day. Longer than three weeks. But her kindness blinded her from seeing the truth. He was damaged goods. Unworthy of her affection. Her grace. He wasn't a turtle she could rehabilitate.

There was no cure for his skin rot.

And that's why he refused to succumb to these feelings. He'd infect her.

Checking his watch, he headed for her bedroom. Time to wake her.

He knocked on her bedroom door. "Little Flynn. It's 0600. Up and at 'em. I'll rustle you up some grub."

A groan sounded behind the door. He grinned and headed to the kitchen. Miss Whittle had already left to have breakfast with the neighbor lady and run errands the rest of the day. Caley finally emerged from the bedroom. Wet head. Glasses. No makeup. The way he liked it.

"Wheezer call?"

"He did."

"I had a feeling. Why else would you wake me?"

"The GoPro was tracked to Palm Lake. We can get the vicinity but not an exact pinpoint."

Caley added some scrambled eggs to her plate and a piece of toast. "That was her favorite place. You think she met up with her killer there?"

"Likely, but I'm not sure what went down or how she lost it—or tossed it." He buttered his toast.

"Thanks for breakfast," she said.

"Welcome."

They ate quietly, then headed for Palm Lake.

"Just park anywhere," Caley said, digging through her purse and retrieving a pair of prescription sunglasses.

Shep pulled into a space near the sidewalk that led into the park. Only a few cars dotted the lot. Bird-watchers. Runners maybe. The sun was bright in the sky already. It was going to be a scorcher, and rain would come fairly soon. The muggy air was pregnant with it.

"It's located somewhere about two miles north of the foot trails." Shep had done research on Palm Lake while sitting up all night. Palm Lake was one of the largest maple swamps on the Gulf coast. The view from their car was amazing. Too bad it wasn't going to be a leisurely stroll. And he wanted to beat the rain.

Caley clambered from the car and stretched. "Gonna rain soon."

Smiling, Shep locked the car and surveyed the parking lot one last time, taking in the details of every vehicle. Watching for danger.

Birds squawked and chirped. "Let's get to it." They walked to the entrance of the park, lined with signs that gave them instructions, warned them of gators and showed pictures of many varieties of birds with blurbs about each. Herons, ibis, eagles, wood storks.

Salt and earth invaded his senses.

The wooden boardwalk led to a covered observation tower. From here, Shep eyed two older gentlemen with binoculars.

"Nature trails start over there." Caley pointed in the direction of the tower and they hoofed it, only to be met by a runner coming out.

"Ashley," Caley exclaimed.

She tore her earbuds from her ears, her sweat-soaked T-shirt and forehead evidence of a good workout. "Hey, Caley. Mr. Lightman."

"You really shouldn't be running alone in a secluded park. It's not safe," he said.

She shrugged off his warning with a smile. "Ah. It's safe out here this early. I run it every morning."

Caley fanned her face. Already the temperature was rising. "Did Mary Beth ever run with you?"

Ashley laughed. "No. But occasionally she'd come with me and bird-watch, shoot photos while I ran." She studied them. "What are you guys doing out here?"

"Nature walk," Shep offered. A gut feeling hit him.

What if she was out here searching for the GoPro? Could she know about it?

"Lots of that here." She checked her phone. "I'm on dive duty this morning, so…"

"Yeah," Caley said. "Go on."

Ashley checked her phone again. "Happy nature walking." She jogged toward the lot.

"Where's she from?" Shep asked.

"Georgia, actually." She took the lead down the path. Trees flanked each side. A grouping of white birds with long legs and beaks tromped around the wetland. "Ibis." Caley acknowledged the birds Shep had been watching.

"I see why Mary Beth liked it out here."

Caley nodded. "There's a place not far from here where she spent most of her time."

Shep walked along beside her. "Is it near the area on the app?" He showed it to her. Wheezer had sent screenshots.

"Yeah. Anything else from Wheezer?"

"Leo Fines's accounts had zero large deposits. But one fairly substantial withdrawal about three days before we saw him carry the black duffel bag into the club."

"You think he was bringing Kyle Marx money? Why? If he was selling eggs…"

"Just because he withdrew a substantial amount of money doesn't mean he was paying anyone off or delivering it to the club. Could still be eggs in that bag," Shep said. They'd never be able to prove that he'd stolen eggs unless Mary Beth had recorded it on the GoPro. "I'd like to see those journal entries Leo Fines has. The ones logging rescued and rehabilitated sea turtles. But asking again will garner another negative response."

"True. We could sneak in there and see if we can find them." Caley studied the edge of the trail and took a left. "That's the grove of wildflowers she loved to shoot."

Red and white ones. Shep had seen them in her photos.

"You think after we inquired about the journals, he'd leave them in his office?" Didn't seem smart. Shep wouldn't have.

"I don't know. Worth a shot." She held her arms out. "Mary Beth loved this spot."

A small area hemmed in by maples. The wildflowers from some of the photos abounded. Red, white, purple. "This place is secluded but not too far off the path. If the killer lured her to this park, I don't see him wanting to be positioned in a more public area."

"Who knows where they met up. We only know the vicinity where she left the GoPro. So let's get looking."

They trekked to the general area. Great. Salt marshes. Caley groaned.

Shep squatted surveying the area, a few wood storks milling about. "A salt marsh. Water. Salt."

Caley frowned, then gasped. "Mary Beth could have been drowned here. Sea water. It's definitely secluded. Let's fan out. We can cover more ground."

Shep blocked her path forward. "What about gators?"

Caley twisted her lips. "It's a possibility they're out here, but typically they stay away from areas of high salinity."

"Typically. But not always." He bent and secured his gun from his ankle holster. "Let's search together."

Caley nodded and trudged into the swampy wetland. Shep's hiking boots were waterproof but only up to his ankles.

They combed the area, starting with the section closest to the water and fanning out from there. After an hour, Shep wasn't so sure they'd find the GoPro. But the app said it was in this area, and it was accurate to within one hundred feet.

Moving back toward the trail, Caley paused. "Hey." She knelt in the long grass and dug below. "I stepped on something." She hollered a victory cry and pumped her fist, GoPro in hand. "We got them now, Shep! We have the proof we need."

*Crack!*

Caley ducked and shrieked as gunfire ensued.

Shep dove toward her, covering her. "Run!"

They bolted through the marsh, water splashing as they traipsed through the wetlands.

Birds blasted through the trees as another shot was fired.

"Take cover in those maples over there!" Shep steered her left and into a thicket of trees.

Caley's breath turned heavy. "We can cut through over there but it's dense."

The shots had been fired from the east. "Is there another nature trail on the side the shots came from?"

"Yeah," Caley said, keeping low. Shep continued to shield her.

Birds taking flight and the sound of the gunfire would lead the bird-watchers to call Fish and Wildlife. Hunting was illegal and that's what they'd assume was happening.

Other than Caley's breathing and the small rustle of leaves, the park was silent.

"Let's push through this. Where will we come out?" he asked.

"Main boardwalk."

Sitting ducks.

Maybe they should call Tom. Bring in some reinforcement. He reached for his phone.

"You won't get a signal out here. Not in these deep marshes. Only near the parking lot."

Well, it was risk bullets or fight possible gators. "Lead the way. I've got your six." Their feet slogged in the muddy waters, grass rising at times to Shep's waist and Caley's torso. But she didn't complain.

"Shep?"

"Yeah."

"What if they're waiting for us at the car?" Fear penetrated through the question. A very good question. One of them might have fired to scare them into running right to the parking lot. Right into a trap.

"Be still. Get low. Here." He shoved her under a thatch of plants. "Don't move. If they're on our tail, he'll fire again when we emerge from the thicket. If not...you might be right." He couldn't be sure how many pursuers were in the area. But he would keep her safe. Reinforcements or not.

Shep slogged through the marsh until he made it to the walking trail and took one step out. Listening, he waited. It was almost 1000 hours. The park would be filling up. Would shooters risk being seen holding them up for a GoPro? Had they seen the GoPro? He'd been paying close attention on the drive over. They hadn't been followed. The whole point of going at daylight was to help secure their safety.

Surely, they wouldn't risk killing them in a public parking lot or they would have fired into the crowd that night at the club.

Unless this was another set of goons after them. He had no choice.

Another step out, a bullet whizzed by his head, splintering bark on the maple tree next to him. He ducked inside the secluded trees and sprinted back to Caley. "They're on to us."

"I heard the shot," she said. "You hurt?"

"No. Let's double back. They'll expect us to keep moving forward. Emerge at the boardwalk."

Back through the foliage, they worked their way to the salt marsh, following the trail that led to the trees lining the parking lot. By the time they made it to the edge of the trees facing the lot, sweat dripped from Shep's temples, his back saturated. Caley looked the same, her cheeks like apples.

He checked his watch. It had been over an hour of pushing through the park to the entrance. The trees opened up to the parking lot. No one by their car. The lot had filled with vehicles and people. Moms with strollers. Couples. Groups of men and women.

Public.

"Let's go." He laced his hand in hers as they jogged to the parking lot, then they walked and stayed close to other people. If someone was out there with a rifle, they wouldn't take the risk.

They wanted that GoPro.

Caley stuck to him like sweaty glue. "Shep, do you think they saw the GoPro? Do you think they know we have it now?"

"The more I think about it, the more my answer is yes. They shot us right after you held it up." These people had planned to take them out, leave them to rot in the swamp or be eaten by a gator. Why not leave Mary Beth out here to meet the same end? They needed the GoPro. They needed Mary Beth's death to look like an accident so the police would stay out of it and they could quietly search.

But now that Shep and Caley had the camera, it didn't matter. Once they had the footage, or photos, they wouldn't care if the police investigated a homicide. The evidence would be in their possession.

Now more than ever Shep couldn't let them get their hands on that GoPro.

Shep hurried Caley inside the car and darted to the driver's side, sliding in and locking the doors.

"Shep?"

"Yeah."

"If we weren't followed, there's only one other explanation."

Shep had been thinking that too.

Only Ashley knew they were here.

# TEN

Caley willed the GoPro to charge faster. Killers knew she had it now. Every pop and creak of the house had her on edge. The rain had started when they left the electronics store, where they'd bought a charger for the GoPro, and it hadn't let up.

It brought a reprieve from the heat, and on a normal day Caley would open the windows for the soothing sound and the breeze to cool the house naturally. Today wasn't a normal day.

Every few minutes Shep would patrol the house, check windows. Thankfully Miss Whittle was gone with Mrs. Bloom, Caley had one less worry.

"You hungry?" Shep asked.

"No. You?"

Caley couldn't eat if she wanted to. But she could sip some warm tea.

"I'm good."

"I can make tea. Would you drink tea?" she asked.

First smirk since they'd made it out of the park by the skin of their teeth. "Probably not."

She padded to the kitchen. Made a cup of chamomile for herself.

"Charged," Shep said as she entered the living room.

Her stomach knotted. What if the murder had been accidentally filmed? Caley couldn't handle that.

When she met Shep's gaze, he nodded. "I'll look at it
first. That okay?"

How did he know what she was thinking? Were her
facial expressions that obvious? Or did he know her better than she realized? He'd risked his life for her again.
Sheltered her like a rock-solid shell. "Thank you," she
whispered.

"No problem. If there's nothing too disturbing I'll—"

"No. I mean for saving me. For being willing to take
a bullet for me. That means a lot, Shep."

He half nodded, still unable to take a compliment.

"You say you aren't good, but you are. You help people. You served our country. That's good. Brave. Self-
sacrificing."

"Caley," he murmured. "Stop."

She froze. "Why?"

He massaged his neck, looked away. "I don't want to
hear any of that."

"But it's true," she insisted.

"Don't make me out to be some hero. I'm just a man
paying penance for my sins. Making it right as best I can."

A burning sensation started in her stomach and rose
clear to her head. He couldn't be telling the truth. That
would make her... No. Just no. The idea of what she was
to him blew her over the edge. "So I'm penance. Another
mission to earn you points with God? You save me, you
win. You don't, then *oh well*? You can try again on another mission."

Fire licked through his eyes, darkening them. "That's
what you think?" The grit in his voice reminded her of
a lion stalking prey, about to pounce. He stood, stepped
toward her.

"What am I supposed to think after that?" She folded

her arms, raised her chin. "Tell me. Am I just a mission? Just Wilder's *baby* sister?" Where was this going? What did she want to hear? That she meant something to him. That he cared about her. Even if he did, she couldn't reciprocate those feelings, yet here she was, pushing for a truth she might not be able to stand hearing.

And she was mad at herself because she already had feelings for Shep. Stronger than she'd ever had for anyone. A solider! This was all wrong.

He invaded her space, tipped her chin and stared at her.

A wave rippled through her middle. "Well?" she choked out.

She couldn't read his dark mood. Turmoil? Longing? He released her chin and shook his head. "I'm going to watch the footage and go through photos. I'll let you know what I find." He stormed to the kitchen without another word.

He wouldn't even fight with her.

She *wanted* a fight. Something. So many emotions piling up. So many questions. About Shepherd. About her feelings for him. She collapsed on the couch and covered her face with a pillow but refrained from screaming into it.

Ten minutes later, Shep entered the living room. "You need to see this."

*Oh no.*

Sitting beside her, he held out the GoPro. "Here's the footage she caught. And our theory wasn't too off. But it wasn't on either."

Caley clutched her stomach and leaned toward Shep to see better. He smelled clean, the scent of his cologne wreaking havoc with her heart. "I'm ready."

He pushed Play and Caley watched in horror.

Billy Reynolds and Darcy Fines—Leo's daughter— digging up turtle eggs and placing them in backpacks.

"Who's the girl? I don't recognize her as an intern."

"Leo Fines's daughter. Darcy." Caley sat slack jawed. Mary Beth had caught them. Filmed them. Probably approached Billy about it. Did she tell him she had footage? "I can't believe this."

"That's not all." Shep stopped the video and scrolled to the photos. Several photos of Billy and Darcy with the backpacks, going into the Nest. One of them with Rob, the bartender.

*Rob!*

"We knew he was in on it. He might be the middleman. And he's the same build as the guy at the beach who tried to drown me." Caley shook her head. "You think she confronted Billy and he went to Leo? Or Rob?"

Shep ran his top teeth along his bottom lip. "Possibly."

Caley wanted to be sick. "Right under my nose? I'm so stupid!"

"You're not stupid, Caley. You're invested in this job. In these people. You see way too much good in everyone," he muttered.

Was that what bothered him? The good she saw in him that he didn't see? Couldn't accept? Wouldn't believe?

She covered her face with her hands and leaned forward.

What she wouldn't give for a hug. A pat. But she'd demanded he not do it again. Not out of duty. And he wouldn't have any reason to otherwise. Her throat tightened.

"What do we do? Take this to Tom?"

Shepherd glared at the GoPro. "It's motive for murder. It might change their minds about it being an accident. But I'd like to talk to Ashley, see who she made calls to this morning—if she'll be honest—and then haul Leo in myself. Right after he confesses. He owes you that, Caley. Truth right to your face. Then we can turn the rest over to Turtle Bay PD, and Tom. Let them make the arrests."

"I want those journals too. He's going to give them to me. I'll be able to detect discrepancies. Then we can turn that in as evidence too."

"I'll make sure he does."

Shep had his ways. "This time of day he'd still be at the office."

"Then let's go. We can't keep waiting for the rain to let up."

Caley's nerves hummed but she needed to confront her mentor. They'd stopped by Ashley's dorm room and questioned her about the park. She admitted she texted Billy Reynolds and made a comment about Caley and her "new boyfriend" together at all times of the day. Caley's cheeks had heated at that innuendo. And she said she'd called Dr. Fines because she had dive duty and was running late.

So both Billy and Leo had time to have either come out or called someone in. More likely, one of them tipped off the club owner because he had goons with guns.

Leo Fines? Wanting her dead? It sunk like a lead weight in her gut. Once Leo confessed, Shepherd would turn over all the evidence to Tom and have him and Billy arrested. Goodbye Arnold Simms Center. Goodbye donors, grants and this life she'd made and loved so much.

What if he didn't confess? Nothing on video connected him to anything. But Shep had the photo of Leo going into the club with the duffel bag. Circumstantial evidence.

She knocked on Leo's office door and opened it.

Leo looked like he hadn't slept in a year. "Now what?" he asked, his voice tired. Defeated.

"We have video footage from Mary Beth's GoPro, Leo. See it for yourself." Caley nodded to Shep, who played the GoPro.

Leo sank in his office chair and ran a hand through his hair.

"We also have proof you took a duffel bag into that club. How could you? How could you sell turtle eggs? You don't want to protect your career by keeping this quiet. You want to protect your criminal activity!" Caley roared, losing all composure and not even caring.

Leo's eyes bugged. "What? You think I poached eggs and... How dare you?"

"Then explain yourself, Leo," Caley said. Shep remained quiet. For now.

"You've got it all wrong." Leo inhaled deeply. "Darcy's been in trouble for a long time. She got tangled up with that horrible Kyle Marx. The club owner."

Caley gave Shep a knowing look. That guy was bad news all around.

"Once she got caught up with him, she got messed up in drugs. Quit grad school. Moved into a condo overlooking the ocean. Who do you think pays for that?"

Kyle Marx.

"What was in that duffel bag?" Shep asked.

Leo shot Shep a glance. "Money. I took a chunk of savings and tried to pay him to leave her alone. He took it and said he'd send her home to me. But he kept the money and nothing's changed." Despair and grief flooded his face. "I didn't know about her involvement in the poaching or Billy's. Not until now." He sunk into his chair. "But I'm not completely surprised."

"Because of what you found in the data? In the journals you wouldn't let me see?" Caley leaned on the desk. "Why are you keeping those journals from me, Leo?"

"Yes. I saw some discrepancies. May tenth we rescued three turtles from longlines. I went out personally. Ashley and Billy were along. And Toby. On the fifteenth, I logged one turtle. Only Billy and Toby were with me that day. When I went back to the data, it showed two turtles rescued on the tenth and none on the fifteenth."

Caley clasped a hand over her mouth. "The books were doctored. To show fewer turtles. Did they think you'd forget?"

"I typically don't deal with the data, but the gala is coming up."

"So you pulled the journals for your speech. Who was responsible?" Caley asked.

"I don't know. I was waiting it out to see if it happened again. See if I could catch the culprit. Then Mary Beth died."

"Because she'd found the same thing," Shep offered. He turned to Caley. "Billy would be the likeliest person she'd go to, don't you think?"

"Not necessarily. She and Ashley were close—and we were shot at after we saw her in the park."

"You were shot at?" Leo asked.

"Yes!" Caley hissed.

Shepherd cocked his head. "Ashley said she called you this morning and mentioned we were there."

"She did. She was running late." Leo's eyes grew wide. "I had nothing to do with your being shot at! I'm just trying to help my daughter."

Ashley could have called Leo and Billy like she said, but she could have also called Kyle Marx directly and left that out. They needed to confront Billy.

Shep ignored Leo. "What about Toby? Remember that photo we found of them? She could have confided in him."

True. But all she could think of was the turtles. Where were those precious creatures now? Tears burned the back of her eyes and flames licked up her belly. "This is why you told me to stop meddling, isn't it, Leo? You knew that if Nora and the donors got wind of this, none of us would work again."

"And I wanted time to figure out who was behind the turtle theft. And to deal with Darcy."

"Is that who you were talking to on Ladies' Night in the office at the Nest? I heard you." Caley shook her head, trying to wrap her brain around all of this.

Leo gaped. "You heard me? How?"

"Doesn't matter. Is that what you were doing there? Talking to Darcy?" Caley asked. Shep continued to burn a hole through Leo with a glare.

"Yes. Once I realized they'd taken my money and she wasn't leaving. He wasn't going to make her." He rested his head on the back of his office chair and closed his eyes. "I knew she was there. I went to talk to her. Her drug use… It is all out of control." Snapping his head to attention, he looked straight at Caley. "But there is no way Darcy had anything to do with murdering Mary Beth. If it even is a homicide. The police still say it was accidental drowning."

"They made it look like that, Leo!"

"Well, Darcy didn't do it! She's messed up with a dangerous man, but she's not a murderer, Caley. You know her." Leo jumped up and paced the floor next to window. "I don't know what to do."

Neither did Caley.

"I want to talk to Billy Reynolds," Shep said. "Different line of questioning. Not so nice. He was the boyfriend, but he was hooked up with Darcy. How did that happen? They're the only two in the footage."

"Darcy is too blinded by Kyle Marx to be romantically involved with Billy. But she does come around often enough that knowing him wouldn't be a stretch."

Caley rubbed her temples. A major headache was coming on. Darcy used Billy to help her deliver eggs to Kyle Marx. It made sense to believe that Billy was also the one doctoring logbooks and stealing turtles.

"If you tip your daughter off about the information we have, he might see her as collateral damage and take you both out. If she's loyal to him, you won't be able to talk her into leaving him. Understand?" Shep narrowed his eyes.

Leo's face turned white, but he nodded. "Darcy made a mistake. I'll deal with her about that. But she's not a murderer. And I want to believe she wouldn't steal turtles to sell on the market."

"She stole eggs, Leo. She stole those babies." Caley inhaled deeply.

Leo's angst matched her own. "I know, Caley. And I'm so sorry. What should I do?"

"Business as usual. Until we talk to Billy Reynolds and get answers. Then it's out of our hands and into TBPD's. I'm sorry that Darcy might go to jail, but what she did was wrong." Caley turned and marched out of his office, only to feel her knees buckle in the hallway.

Shep steadied her. "This okay?" he whispered.

The feel of his arms holding her upright never felt better. She nodded.

"We're getting closer, Caley, and now you can keep an eye on the turtles. Make sure no more are stolen."

"But where are the ones that were taken? And what if Leo tips off Darcy anyway?"

"He won't. He's hoping this will all go away and donors won't catch wind. But that's probably not going to happen. You know that, right?"

She did. But they still had a gala to put on and there was still hope that if they brought justice to the turtles it would prove how much they loved them. And maybe with the reassurance that they'd vet potential interns more intensely in future, they could keep going. Hang on.

"Let's visit Billy Reynolds before I update Wilder and Tom." Shep popped the umbrella at the door and they took cover from the torrential rain. "Maybe the weather will ease up by then too."

Caley was fairly sure nothing was going to ease up anytime soon.

# ELEVEN

After leaving Leo Fines's office, Shepherd and Caley tried to track down Billy Reynolds, but he wasn't at the center, the dormitory or at any of the dive sites. So was he simply off doing his own thing or had he figured out they had the GoPro and bolted? Either way, Shepherd had called Tom and filled him in. He was now looking into it officially.

Shep downloaded all the footage and photos from the GoPro and emailed them to Wheezer while Caley made a dinner that consisted of noodles and tuna. Wasn't half bad minus the mushrooms. Miss Whittle wouldn't be home until bedtime, which was good all around. Someone would be coming again, no doubt. He'd debated moving both the women from the house, but staying here in the bungalow actually gave Shepherd an advantage. He knew the layout and had purchased a few cameras from an electronics store. Perimeters had been set up. He was ready for them.

Now he was stretched on the futon in Caley's office. It smelled like her. Flowery. A little fruity. He'd been wracking his brain to find a way to keep this quiet and to save her career, but once they cracked this wide-open, it would make headlines. The town was small. The center was a major tourist attraction. He only hoped the media and the civilians would see that Caley had been dedicated to finding the truth.

Turmoil twisted inside him. What was this? The opening up of his personal life. The physical contact coming easier, almost naturally, like gaining hold of her in the hallway. It had been instinct to buoy her. And the ferocious need to keep her safe, to be near her, was overwhelming. He inhaled the scent on her decorative pillow lying next to him. What was up with that? He was smelling pillows now?

He needed to get it together.

Caley Flynn was off-limits. That's why he'd put a stop to her monologue about his bravery, goodness and sacrifice for country and clients. She said every word with conviction and it was unraveling a cord in Shep that needed to stay coiled. Tight. He couldn't let her words connect with his heart.

One, it was hard to believe. And the minute he made a mistake in front of her, she'd see it wasn't true and abandon him.

Two, Wilder would never have it. And he wouldn't disobey a direct order. Even if Wilder was his friend, he was also his boss.

How could Caley think she was nothing more than a mission? He'd wanted to shake some sense into her. Kiss it into her. Each day it was getting harder to keep her at arm's length.

But he hadn't given her any indication to believe something else. Not really.

Let her think she was a mission. A favor to her brother. It would be easier that way. Easier to disconnect. To keep up the wall that was crumbling so fast his head spun.

Frustration built in his chest and he grabbed the Bible lying on the side table. Caley's Bible. He flipped through it, a rainbow of highlighted passages meeting him with each flip.

A woman who loved God's word. Cared about doing the right thing. Not for penance or to prove she was worthy, but because she knew she was loved no matter what. And because she was just good.

He paused on a pink highlighted passage.

*But God shows His great love for us in this way: Christ died for us while we were still sinners.*

He noticed a note in the margin written in Caley's handwriting: "Thank You, God, for loving me even though I'm not perfect and sin daily."

Caley Flynn? Sin daily? At all?

Chaplain Chastain always said, "All people sin. If we say we don't sin, we're deceiving ourselves." He couldn't quite remember what scripture that came from.

But Caley's sins couldn't hold a candle to Shep's. His were greater. His wild lifestyle. Stealing. Lies. Hatred. The random fights where he'd hurt people. The list could go on and on. He hadn't been that man in years, but he couldn't help but think that God might change His mind about Shep. Cut him loose at some point.

The knock on the door frame startled him. Caley stood there, questions in her eyes.

He held up her Bible. "You don't mind me reading this, do you?"

"No. Of course not." She padded inside and plopped beside him. His first instinct was to draw her to his chest and hold her. Make her feel safe. And to feel content himself. "What are you reading?"

"The one about God loving us even when we were still sinning."

"One of my favorites. Dying on the cross. The ultimate act of love. Knowing every sin we'd ever commit. And doing it anyway." Her eyes took on a dreamy expression.

Shep shifted on the couch, faced her. He had to know. "Caley, what are your sins?"

She removed her glasses and rubbed her eyes. "A man who would rather crawl into a hole than open up to me wants me to open up to him?"

She had a point. But he wanted to know everything about her. The good. The bad. The ugly. If there was any bad or ugly to be found. And that was strange and new for him. He'd never cared to get to know a woman emotionally. But Caley Flynn was no ordinary woman. "Sorry. That was too personal."

She rubbed her lips together and gave him a soft smile. "I hated Meghan's murderer. Wouldn't forgive him. For one."

"Seems justified."

"But it's not." Caley took the Bible from Shep, flipped through the pages. "'Love your enemies,' *Luke* 6:27." She flipped again. "'But if you don't forgive other people, then your Father in heaven will not forgive your sins.'"

"You forgave him?"

"I did. Some days I'm tempted, though. To let that hate resurface. Takes a lot of prayer and focus. And I was mad at God for allowing it to happen. But now, I'm not so much mad as I am sad she's gone, and confused."

"I was mad at God for a long time. Before I finally gave my life to Him. Mad that He gave me a loser father who didn't even care enough to let me know who he was. And mad because my mom was a junkie who mostly worked stripping. Mad that a good family didn't want me. Even when I acted out. I was just really, really mad."

Caley grinned. "Shepherd Lightman. You just opened up to me and I didn't even have to put a gun to your head or ask you to."

He had no idea what to make of that.

"I'm sorry you never felt wanted or loved. But God always wanted you. Always loved you. Look how strong you are because of what you went through. God molded you through those tragic events. But even so..." She melted him with her compassion. Those watery blues connecting with his, reaching into the depths of who he was, to his insecurities.

"Even so what?" he rasped, aching to kiss her. Not for the need of physical contact. He wanted to connect with her heart, show her...what? What was this feeling? It terrified him.

"Even so, I'm sorry. I'm just so very sorry." She scooted up on her knees and wrapped her arms around his neck, clinging to him. Pouring warmth and hope into his soul.

"I thought you said no physical contact."

"Well, this one is warranted. Out of...friendship. Not duty."

He paused, but then he embraced her around the waist, drawing her even closer, her scent undoing him. But not as much as her gesture. He'd been gruff, and even downright mean and rude to her, and here she was always coming back. Always showing him grace. Forgiveness.

But for how long?

Shep could love this woman. If he had any idea how.

She snuggled closer, burrowing her nose into his neck, sending shivers down his back as her lips innocently grazed his skin. "I don't want to be a mission, Shep."

He swallowed the lump in his throat. "What *do* you want, Caley?" He had nothing to give.

She pulled away, gazed into his eyes, kept her hands cupped around his neck. Confusion. Pain. Fear. All surfaced in her eyes like a wave, tears building. "I don't know," she whispered. She blinked, the tears spilled over and she let go of his neck, removed herself from him, from the futon, and turned away. "I need to go out to the beach by the center tonight. Since it's stopped raining. Check the nest sites."

"Okay." He wouldn't press her. It was hopeless. He set the Bible back on the side table. "Just say when you're ready to go."

She nodded and slipped from the room.

Leaving him.

A foreshadowing of what would come if he threw caution to the wind and gave it a go. Gave his heart to her. Seemed like she might already own it.

Caley dusted the sand from her backside, covering her wrist to hide the light while checking her watch for the time. After 11:00 p.m. They'd logged eggs and done a few rounds keeping vehicles off the beach. Tourists mostly ignored the signs. It was a hassle every nesting season. A few eggs had hatched, but the bulk would happen in a few weeks.

"Is this boring you?" she asked.

"No, it's kinda cool."

She snickered. "See those tracks from the beach to here? A turtle came to lay eggs."

"But I don't see any eggs. Animals get to them?"

Caley knelt. "No. It's what we call a false crawl. The turtle more than likely came up to dig a nest and lay eggs, but headlights or lights from windows confused her and she thought she made a mistake, so she went back out to sea."

"Can you tell what kind of turtle it was?" Shep asked.

Caley nodded.

"How?"

"The flipper pattern. The tracks alternate. Like footprints. And they're about thirty-six inches so this particular turtle was a loggerhead. I hate it for her. Can you imagine dragging through sand on flippers, at two hundred pounds? Lot of work. Only to be confused by lights." Caley sighed.

"You really love this, don't you?"

"I do. And I'm probably going to end up blackballed in this profession when it all comes to light." What else was out there for her?

"Does the lady over this center really have that kind of power?"

"Yes. Arnold Simms was famous in marine biology. Do you know most marine life vets have to work their way into a position like I have? Leo went out of his way to get me here. I'll never find another job like this."

"Maybe we hope for the best."

*We.* She would love to have a husband who was her partner in hope. Carried some of the load. But it couldn't be Shepherd. She'd almost tossed her promise to herself out the window in her office earlier. What if he'd admitted he cared about her? What would she have done with that? Which is why when he'd asked her what she wanted, she'd told him she didn't know. Because she didn't. And she did.

She couldn't endure the pain and worry of loving a soldier. Already, he'd been willing to take bullets for her, put his life in danger countless times. And he did that for anyone he was instructed to. One day he might not dodge the bullet. Might not make it across one roof to another. Or out of a salt marsh.

Caley had to get a handle on her feelings.

*God, I'm in trouble here because...I think I'm falling in love with this soldier man who is unsure of who he is and has a hard time opening up...and You've seen his comforting tactics. But I can't love him. So help me. Take away these feelings.*

Shep brushed the sand from his jeans. "I want to check on Billy Reynolds again, see if he's back at the dormitory, unaware that we're on to him, that Tom is on the hunt for him too. He might be willing to cough it all up and confess given some incentive."

Scary incentive.

"Then what?"

"If he confesses, he goes to jail for more than digging up and selling sea turtle eggs. And you hold the gala anyway. Unless you're told not to."

"Like you said, I can only hope for the best. Try to trust God to work for me. One way or the other."

They walked next door and Caley unlocked the doors, then entered the dormitory. She knocked on Billy's door. No answer. "We don't have curfews, as you know, but it's late. For a Wednesday night." She knocked again and turned the door knob. It opened.

The room was dark. "He might be out."

Shep frowned. "He's been gone since we found the GoPro. I don't like it."

Caley only hoped he hadn't been tipped off and fled. He couldn't go far. Tom and the TBPD would find him— and Darcy Fines and Kyle Marx now that they had the footage in their possession. "I don't like it either."

Back outside, Caley yawned and stretched. "Sometimes checking nests kills my back."

"You haven't had much sleep. Tonight, you need to rest. I'll keep watch."

"I know you will," she murmured. "Thank you. But I need to check my emails and see if the grant came through."

"Check it now."

"I can't. Light. Even the smallest source makes a difference." She walked along the beach, heading for the center.

"If you get the grant, what does it mean?" Shep asked.

"New lab equipment. Funds to update tanks and increase our staff. Put a new marine life vet on board. It means a lot. If we can keep them from pulling out when they find out turtles and eggs have been grossly mishandled." Her joy deflated. She didn't see any way around this. "I appreciate you, Shep, being quiet and working with Tom at the Turtle Bay Police Department to skirt around the media."

"It won't stay quiet once everyone is found and questioned. Once truth starts coming out."

"Just say 'you're welcome' okay?" She playfully punched his arm as they strolled down the beach, neither mentioning they'd passed the center twenty feet back.

"You're welcome."

They walked a little farther. The tide was high. The water raced across their bare feet. "We should get back. Tomorrow is going to be jam-packed with overseeing the setup for the gala."

They doubled back. A light flashed. Turning, Caley shielded her eyes from the blinding lights. A spotlight? Headlights?

The rev of an engine sent her pulse skittering.

A huge lifted four-wheel-drive truck raced right for them.

"Run!" Shep hollered.

Caley made a dash for the water but Shep yanked her away. "They have us if we go in the water. They can sit out here and wait." They blasted across the beach, the truck gaining on them. Her calves burned as she ran in the powdery sand, shells cutting into her bare feet. "Up ahead!"

They charged up the beach, hoping for cover among the condos and businesses that lined the shore. The truck sprayed sand.

Caley's breath came in pants. She was desperate for air but adrenaline kept her legs moving at a pace she'd never imagined she could go.

Shep looked back, dove onto Caley, knocking them forward and landing them a few feet away with a thud.

Shep rolled them under a raised boardwalk leading to a condominium's private pool area.

Under the boardwalk, shells and debris cut into Caley's back. Shep hovered over her, shielding her, his weight pressing against her.

The truck's engine grew quieter until it couldn't be heard anymore. Only her ragged breath, Shep's even breathing and the sound of ocean waves. She touched her face. Her glasses were missing. Must have been hurled off in the tackle. A tackle that had saved their lives.

Reality set in and she shivered underneath the warmth of Shep's body. "They were going to mow us down. That was no scare tactic."

Sweeping a mass of hair from her face, Shep's eyes blazed. "They know you have the GoPro. They probably assume you have taken or will take it to the authorities, exposing them."

Caley closed her eyes. "Which means I'm expendable. Get me out of the way permanently and deal with the aftermath later."

"Not gonna happen, Caley. I won't let it."

"Shepherd?"

"Yeah?"

"Duty or not. I need some physical contact." She was about to lose it. Knowing someone wanted her dead sent a sweeping wave of nausea over her.

Shep pulled her to an upright position and guided her into his arms. "Caley, we're going to finish this. I promise." He stroked her hair, tightened his hold on her. "I won't leave you until I know you're safe and whoever is behind this is brought down. You can count on me."

That was her problem. She was counting on him too much. When he finished the job, he'd leave.

# TWELVE

The sun had risen two hours ago and Caley sat in the sand with her knees drawn up.

After they'd returned to Caley's, she'd checked her email. They'd gotten the grant. She wanted to leap for joy, but none was to be found. The grant might get yanked. And a killer was coming for her.

But Shepherd had promised to protect her. To keep watch. Even now he was watching from her patio. But Caley couldn't make herself venture down to the water's edge. It was too soon after almost being drowned in it.

These monsters had turned her safe haven into a living nightmare. The one place she loved most, felt the safest, was now a place where she'd almost lost her life. A place Shep had almost lost his. *Help us, God. Help us get through this alive.*

It was almost eight o'clock now. She still had to go to the center and do some last-minute prep work before she arrived at the dormitory to set up for the gala by ten.

She ached for rest.

For peace.

Ached as she remembered being in Shep's embrace. Though she'd asked for it, it had come naturally. No hint of awkwardness. No hesitation. As if he'd been hugging her his whole life. As if he wanted to continue for the rest of it. Yet he was leaving after she was safe. At least she had him for now.

"It's going to be a beauty of a day today, isn't it?" Miss Whittle padded over, an album in her hand, and sat beside Caley. "Shepherd cleaned the breakfast dishes and folded the blanket on the couch. I've never seen a blanket folded so perfectly. Other than my JC. He was a military man through and through. Like your Shepherd."

Caley rested her head on her knees. "Miss Whittle, Shep is not mine."

"Oh, but I think he is."

She heaved a breath. "I can't be with a soldier. A man who does what Shepherd does every day. I can't. I watched my grandma and so many others go through the pain. I refuse to live in a constant state of worry. I can't have him ripped from me. My heart wouldn't be able to take it."

Miss Whittle grunted.

"What's that mean?" Caley asked, raising her head.

"Today would have been my sixtieth anniversary had JC lived. We married young. So in love. He joined the military and went to war. You want to talk about worry? I worried."

But Miss Whittle didn't seem anything like Gran after Gramps died. She wasn't depressed, and Gran never spoke of anniversaries. It was too hard on her. "Miss Whittle. I'm so sorry you lost the love of your life to war."

"Not to war, dear. Not even to the dangers of his job when he left the military. He became a Fish and Wildlife officer. Poachers. Animals. Always something to worry about. And we had some doozies of fights in our early years. I wanted him to be safer."

That seemed fair. Justified.

"God taught me a valuable lesson. We aren't here forever. But while we are, He wants us to live for Him however He chooses. And that's what my JC did. He served

God by serving the country and the people of this great state. He was a hero." Miss Whittle opened the album, flipped through a few pages. Wedding. The birth of their son. Dances. Birthdays. Graduation. Vacations. Holidays.

Caley laid a hand on her swooning heart. "He loved you. That's obvious. The way he looks at you in those pictures."

"The way Shepherd looks at you, dear. Are you blind or avoiding it because you're too afraid to risk telling him that you love him? Because I also see the way you look at him."

Caley had been ignoring it. Calling it strong feelings but the truth was she did love Shepherd as hard as she'd tried not to. What was she going to do with that? "I don't want to get hurt. I don't want to be a widow too young. I don't want...to risk the pain."

"Well, who does?" Miss Whittle snorted. "Look out there." She pointed to the immense ocean. "It's in the deep waters you really learn to trust God."

"You also have nowhere to go if the boat sinks."

"I believe I remember a young disciple who got out in the deep and started to sink. Seems Someone was instantly there to grab his hand, to keep him from going under."

"You're talking about Peter and Jesus."

"So I am. I also remember Jesus once telling Peter to launch out into the deep and let his net over. When he did, do you know what happened?" Miss Whittle asked.

"So many fish filled the net it nearly sank the boat."

"But the boat didn't sink. And if Peter hadn't gone out like Jesus asked, he'd have never experienced the glory of God in an astonishing way. And neither will you."

Caley wiped a tear. "But trusting God doesn't mean safety. Meghan trusted Him and died."

Miss Whittle rubbed Caley's hand. "She also trusted Him and lived."

True. She'd fallen for Beckett, knowing how dangerous his job was. She'd planned a wedding, but it never happened. At least she'd loved. Taken chances. Lived. Caley had crawled into a shell. A lonely shell.

"God's perspective on a safe life isn't the same as ours, Caley. But He's faithful. And always with us."

Meghan might be dead on earth but she was living in heaven. Like Shepherd said. Not an end so much as a new beginning.

Miss Whittle caressed the album's cover. "You know, in the end, I lost JC to cancer. If the good Lord waits a hundred more years to return, there's no way any of us are getting out of here alive. We could die in a car accident tomorrow." Miss Whittle took Caley's hand in a firm grasp. "Don't let fear rob you of loving someone and being loved. 'Cause loving someone…well, honey, that's the best kind of living. That's like walking on water. Get out there. Trust God to hold your hand if your faith sinks."

Miss Whittle kissed Caley's forehead and grunted until she was finally standing. "I love you, honey. You're the daughter I never had. Now stop being so stupid and tell that man how you feel." She gave a solid nod and moseyed back to the house.

What if Miss Whittle was wrong and he didn't feel the same way about her? What if he rejected her? He'd said he wasn't the right man for her. She'd overheard him tell Wilder he wasn't interested in her. But what if he was just scared too? What if fear was holding him back?

Could she muster the strength to commit, to trust, knowing he could lose his life on the job? Miss Whittle had lost her husband and was full of grace and even joy. Her faith had gotten her through the hard times. And she had albums of wonderful memories. Caley wanted albums of wonderful memories too. She wanted those moments where she walked on deep waters.

She wanted to take the chance. Come out of her shell. She was tired of sitting on the edge of the bank like that turtle the day she freed him. She couldn't think about the fear of rejection. Or what words she'd use. She had a gala to plan, a killer to dodge and find, and a grant to hold on to.

Caley stood in the dormitory. The gala event was being held in the old ballroom from when the place had been a motel. She hadn't wanted to set anything up on the beach. Not during nesting season. The room looked lovely. Lights had been strung. A string quartet had arrived and set up. The guests' senses would be flooded with fresh flowers, waterfall fountains and a beautiful summer evening. But she needed to run next door to the center for a few things, including her dress, which she'd left hanging on the door to her office.

Leo had stayed holed up in his office. Avoiding her no doubt. He did mention when she bumped into him in the center's hall that Darcy hadn't called and wouldn't return any of his calls. They went to voice mail. She was avoiding him.

Or something sinister had happened.

To both Billy and Darcy. They would be collateral damage for Kyle Marx as much as Caley was.

Shepherd had kept his distance most of the day while she instructed the setup crew and caterers, but she'd never been out of his line of sight. Wasn't out of his sight even now, as he stood near the door to the ballroom wearing black dress pants and a white dress shirt. Must have had those packed for evenings on the cruise he'd missed because of her. She'd been pondering everything Miss Whittle had said. She had to face rejection. Face uncertainty.

She had to reveal the truth to Shepherd about how she felt. But she wanted to dress for the gala first.

She met him at the doors. "I need to go next door and change. I brought my clothes but I know you won't let me go alone. Stand outside my office door?"

"On your six." Turmoil swam in his eyes. Maybe his distance and being quieter than normal wasn't just about staying out of her way today.

"Is everything all right, Shepherd?"

He pursed his lips. "Yeah. Yeah. Sure."

She stepped closer, laid a hand on his chest. "You'd tell me if something was wrong, wouldn't you? We've been through a lot these past weeks. I think we can be honest with each other, right? No holding back."

He nodded. "Of course." The words seemed weak.

They walked to her office and he stayed outside the door. "Go get dressed up, Little Flynn."

"The kind of dressed up that makes you think you need to break arms?" *Tell me how you feel, Shepherd! Give me a sign I'm not about to come back and make a monster mistake.*

A faint smile reached his lips. "Go on," he whispered. "I'll be here when you come out."

She wanted him to always be here, but a sense of dread squeezed in her chest. "You promise?"

"You have my word." He leaned around her and opened the office door, his nearness buckling her knees.

Twenty-five minutes later, she donned her sleeveless red dress that dusted the ground. She'd scooped her hair all to one side, where it hung over her shoulder in soft waves. And she'd painted her lips red. Going for that Hollywood Golden Age look.

She opened the office door, stepped out. Shepherd pushed himself off the wall he'd been leaning on, his gaze sweeping over her, connecting with her eyes. He blinked quickly, said nothing.

"Well?" She spun in a slow circle, holding her arms out. Once she faced him, she smiled, but her mouth had turned dry and her hands clammy. "Not so Little Flynn, huh?" *Give me some kind of sign I'm not going to make an idiot of myself, Shepherd.*

He licked his lips. "No. You're stunning, Caley. In a dress. In running shorts. In sweats. Makeup. No makeup." He shrugged. "Doesn't matter."

So he was attracted to her. She moved until the tips of her shoes touched his. "What does matter to you, Shepherd?" *Do I?*

"What do you mean?" He messed with his earlobe and cleared his throat, but he didn't back up.

She cocked her head, held his gaze. Now or never. He had to know how she felt. Time to walk on water and hope she didn't sink. Time to trust God if she did. Time to live. Her stomach quivered. "Shep, I need to tell you something. Something I should have told you days ago."

"No need to say anything, Little Flynn. We're square." His jaw ticked.

"No." She frowned. He had to let her speak. Was he afraid or was he keeping her from embarrassment? "I *need* to tell you—"

"I'm leaving," he blurted. "In about an hour."

His words struck her with force. Leaving? "Are you going to the police department? A lead on Billy or Darcy?" Surely he didn't mean leaving for good. Leaving *her.* Panic jolted through her veins and her lungs constricted.

He glanced away, his neck flushing. "Wilder called earlier on one of his layovers. He's taking over and I'm going on my cruise. You'll be safe with him." He rubbed his chest.

"I'm safe with you!" She didn't want Wilder. She wanted Shepherd.

"You'll be *safer* with him."

Tears betrayed her and surfaced. She shook her head. "You don't believe that. Why are you doing this? How can you just go on a cruise when someone's trying to kill me?" Her voice rose. She didn't care. "And don't say because Wilder will be here! You promised to stick this out to the end, to see it through."

Remaining stoic, he continued to rub at his chest while she searched his eyes. Hollow. Vacant. Unreadable. "Say something," she pleaded. "You owe me an explanation."

He inhaled sharply, his chest rising, jaw working overtime.

He might not have anything to say, but she did. She didn't care if he didn't want to hear it. He was going to. She wasn't going to be ruled by what-ifs. A tear slipped down her cheek, her throat tightened. "I need you to stay. I need *you*, Shepherd... I...*love* you," she whispered. "Please don't go," she begged.

Shepherd closed his eyes, let out a long, slow breath, shoved his hands into his pockets. "It's time."

That was it. Was he not even going to address the fact that she'd bared her heart, laid it all out there? "I guess you were right when you said you weren't the guy for me. Because a man who would leave me when I need him most..." She squared her shoulders, masking her vulnerability, the excruciating pain going on inside her. "You lied to me, Shepherd. You said I could count on you. And you're abandoning me."

His Adam's apple bobbed as he swallowed and looked away.

"*Three weeks*. Sounds about right," she spat as she stormed by him. Sticking around wasn't his thing. He'd said it all along. But she'd thought maybe…maybe she was different. That he might feel differently about her.

He didn't bother to chase after her. To tell her she was worth more than three weeks. Worth anything at all. Miss Whittle had it all wrong. Maybe she had cataracts. Caley exited the center, rushed down the boardwalk and to the beach barefoot, her dress dragging in the sand. He wasn't too far away; he wouldn't abandon his post. Just her.

Her lungs constricted. She felt fevered. Achy. This must be what pneumonia felt like. *Lord, I took a chance and sank. I tried to live but I feel like I've drowned. So help me. Hold my hand and get me through these tidal waves of pain. He doesn't love me back. He doesn't even want to stay. I mean nothing to him. Nothing! And he means everything to me!*

She doubled over and grabbed for air.

Shepherd's arm grasped her upper arm to buoy her. She jerked away, unable to bear his touch. "I don't need any physical contact," she said with more force than intended. The pain was speaking for her.

He released her. "Are you hurt? Sick?"

Did a broken heart count? Did this have no bearing on his heart at all?

She turned her back on him. Couldn't look into his eyes, see the rejection. "Give me some space. I need space." She heaved a breath. "And when you leave," she murmured, "don't offer me a goodbye. Just go."

"Caley," Shepherd croaked. "I—"

"Caley!" Leo waved. "It's time to start."

She marched into the dormitory and into the ballroom, toward the podium, slipping on her shoes and wiping her face, hoping her mascara wasn't running. She nodded at Nora and took her seat next to Leo. He stood and opened the gala with a load of statistics, and then Caley shared the good news about the grant and introduced Nora Simms, daughter of Arnold Simms. Nora hugged Caley. "I'm proud of you, Caley. I know putting this gala together was tough this year since you lost an intern. I'm so sorry."

"Thank you, Nora." *But you don't know the half of it.* And once she did, all this would be washed out to sea.

Nora publicly thanked Leo and Caley for their outstanding service to the community and her late father for his lifetime achievements in the field of marine life. It garnered a huge applause.

Caley wanted to be anywhere but here. She glanced around for Shep. He stood at the back of the room, by the waterfall fountain. After Nora's speech, live music played. Food and drinks flowed. And Caley was required to mingle.

Toby waved from a dessert table.

Caley waved back and he made his way over. "Great job with this."

"Thanks."

"Hey, did you ever get those missing journals back?"

"No. Leo said he was using them for the statistics in his speech. Did you hear all those?" She forced a grin.

"Yeah. I did."

"By any chance have you seen Billy?" Toby roomed right across the hall from him.

"No. I was just gonna ask you the same question. This whole summer has been weird to say the least." He shook his head. "Do you think now that the statistics part of the speech is over, I could get those journals back? I haven't logged them yet and I wanted to get a jump before the turtles start hatching and new data is collected."

He had a point. "I'll see what I can do." She doubted there'd be any point in logging the journals. Not if Nora shut them down. Donors pulled out. The grant that had come through late last night was revoked. She needed air.

Weaving through guests, she exited the gala and headed down toward the beach.

A hand grabbed her arm. "Hey!"

"Ease up, kiddo."

Wilder.

Here to take over.

"Where is Shepherd? He's supposed to be keeping an eye on you." He surveyed the crowd that had spread into the courtyard outside the dormitory. Caley pointed about twenty feet away. Shep was on the beach alone, watching but giving her the space she'd asked for.

"You look terrible," Caley said. "And stop calling me kiddo!"

Wilder frowned. "I've been on a cramped plane for seventy-two hours. What's your excuse for being a crank? And why is my number one guy clear over there while you're roaming around? I could have been the killer." He yanked her along, stalking toward Shepherd. "I'm about to find out," he grumbled. "I can tell you that."

"You *are* acting like a deranged killer." She got out from under his brotherly grip and traipsed along beside him as he stomped to Shepherd.

Wilder stopped short in front of Shepherd, his neck and ears a deep shade of red and his hands balled into fists at his side. He aimed a hard glare at Shep and thumbed toward Caley. "I just intercepted your *asset*," he hissed.

"I'm well aware, but since you're her brother I didn't see the need to put a bullet in you or give chase."

Wilder's emerald green eyes smoldered. "If you'd given chase, you'd have lost."

Shepherd raised an eyebrow. "Doubt that."

Wilder inhaled, lips pursed. "She could have died."

*"She,"* Caley howled, "is right here listening to you bozos argue when you're on the same side! What is wrong with you? Both of you?"

Wilder whirled on her. "You've been attacked repeatedly! A truck almost ran you over. He's supposed to be protecting you better than that." He pointed an accusing finger at Shepherd.

Shepherd bristled.

"I'm alive because of him." She took a breath. Calmed down. Wilder was overprotective, especially after losing Meghan. Fear was driving him. He wasn't really angry at Shepherd. He'd called him his number one. He loved him like a brother. "He's done everything to ensure my physical safety." He'd murdered her heart.

Shepherd narrowed his eyes, cocked his head. Just like the night she'd been mad but offered him a sandwich anyway. She wasn't going to falsely throw him under the bus because he didn't return her feelings.

"But you could have been killed." He turned on Shep. "Why weren't you on her like glue?"

Every emotion that had been shaken in the past two hours blew, and tears sprang in her eyes. The last thing she wanted was to appear to be a weak, sniveling female, but she was broken. Tears turned to sobs. "Because I said I needed space from him. Because he'd rather be a on a cruise than with me. So sue me! And now I need it from you!" She turned in a fury and headed toward the center.

"Caley," Shepherd hollered.

She glanced back, but Wilder had blocked his path, a hand planted firmly on Shep's chest. "What did you do to my sister? I told you not to hurt her!" Wilder continued to drill Shep with a death glare.

Too late. And Caley didn't have time to stick around and listen. She had to pull it together, then she planned to get those logbooks from Leo. She marched up the boardwalk, swung open the center door. Something hard jabbed her ribs.

"You're not going anywhere." Rob from the bar had a

gun to her side. On the other side of her was the bouncer who'd held her hostage at the club. "Anywhere but with us," he said, shoving her around the building.

A black sedan was parked near the front door.

The bouncer opened the back door and shoved her inside. Rob slid in beside her. Gun aimed at her. "Someone wants to have words with you, *Meg.* Isn't that the name you used?"

Shepherd stood at attention while he took his Alpha Charlie from Wilder.

*Three weeks. Sounds about right.*

The blow of Caley's earlier words had landed in his gut. His heart. Like all his bones were shattering and his chest was imploding. He'd rubbed at it ever since, and still the pain wouldn't leave. He'd loosened the two buttons on his shirt, as if it'd help him breathe, but it hadn't worked because Caley was oxygen and she was gone, leaving him to suffocate.

Alone.

Wilder had called late last night to let Shepherd know he was on his way, and Shep had been conflicted. He didn't want Wilder to come. He wanted to see it through. Like he'd said he would. For once. But he didn't tell Wilder that. Fear had won out. Fear that if he stayed he'd fall off the pedestal Caley had put him on. Afraid he'd fail her. Prove he wasn't worthy of a woman of her caliber.

And he'd done exactly that.

She'd come face-to-face with the man he truly was.

A man he wished he wasn't. He pawed his face and ground his jaw.

Caley Flynn loved him. Needed him. God only knew why. Even just now she'd defended him. Though he'd caught her remark about *physically* keeping her safe.

Emotionally, he'd wrecked her. He'd wrecked himself too.

She'd stood before him in a gorgeous red dress and lips painted crimson. He'd wanted to lace his hands through that thick dark hair. Kiss those lips. Promise to keep her safe and secure. She'd laid it all out on the line and his insides had caved in.

Her watery blue eyes had been like daggers piercing his skin. Honest. Vulnerable. Hopeful. Then destroyed.

As she'd slipped away down the boardwalk, his eyes had burned and filled with moisture.

And he had stood there a shell of a man.

*I need you.*

*I love you.*

*Please don't go.*

He was coming apart at the seams; every rip and tear killing him even now as Wilder continued to waste a reprimand on him. "Are you listening?" Wilder snapped his fingers in front of Shep's face.

No, he was trying to keep his 240 pounds of bone and muscle standing upright.

"Did you hear me? Why does she need space? Why is she crying like a puppy? Is something going on between you two?"

"No." Shep shook his head. "That's *why* she needs her space, if you gotta know. Because she does want something from me." And he wanted to give her everything she asked for and more. But couldn't.

Caley couldn't love him. She was confused. Had to be.

"What is she thinking?" Wilder raked a hand through his hair.

Exactly.

"You haven't committed to a woman in the twelve years I've known you! You can't do that to her. She's special."

His blood ran hot, the pain of it all searing through him like an electrical storm. "You think I don't know that?" he barked. "You think I'd treat your sister with anything less than respect? And when did you become her daddy? Last I checked she had one." He'd moved into Wilder's personal space. "You shouldn't even have a say in who she sees or who she doesn't see. I don't need your blessing, Flynn."

Wilder put a finger near Shep's nose. "First off, get out of my face. Second, she's only twenty-six! She's a baby."

"She's not a baby. She's a grown woman. And I *love* her!" he shouted, then stumbled backward stunned at his own admission, but he'd never spoken truer words. His fight dissolved and he couldn't catch his breath. These feelings he couldn't put to words, was too afraid to… *Love.* That's what this was. And he'd let it walk away, slip through his fingers.

No, he'd walked away.

Like he always did.

Shepherd *had* abandoned her.

Done exactly what he feared most.

Proving he was everything he'd ever been told he was.

Pathetic.

Worthless.

Hopeless.

Rotten.

"Why do you think I walked away? I *know* I'm no good for her."

If Wilder realized how much pain Shep had just caused his sister, he'd throw down right here on this beach. Fire him. Turn his back on him.

Like Caley had earlier when she wouldn't let him touch her. It had scared him half to death seeing her bent over at the knees on the beach. Knowing he'd done it.

When she told him to leave without a goodbye.

*Goodbye.*

His stomach roiled. He'd walked away from so many. But this woman… This woman had ruined him for anyone or anything else.

How could he continue to work for Wilder, knowing he'd have to see her on occasion? Maybe someday with another man. His knees nearly buckled at the thought.

He swallowed the mountain of emotion clogging his airway, blinked back the stinging pain.

Wilder stood wide-eyed, equally stunned. Face pale. Jaw to the sand.

"And I'm quitting." He had to. He'd book that cruise. Sail away. Exist somewhere else.

Wilder gave his head a good shake, eyes still foggy. "What? I know I've been hard on you, and this argument—"

"Has nothing to do with it." He turned to give Caley one last look. But she wasn't in their line of sight anymore. "Where's Caley?"

Growling, Wilder sprinted toward the crowd, Shep right beside him, heart thudding against his ribs. They burst into the center, rushed to the door that led to the offices and lab. Empty.

"I can't believe it. We let her out of our sight. This is my fault," Wilder said.

"It's mine." Shep punched a wall and they rushed into the aquarium.

Toby was inside feeding turtles. "Hey, Dr. Fines is looking for you."

"Why?" Shepherd asked.

"I don't know but he seemed upset." He shrugged.

They raced out back and down the boardwalk. Guests mingled as if nothing were wrong. Leo rushed from the dormitory. "I've been looking for you." He did a double take at Wilder. "I was in my office when one of those bouncers from the club forced Caley into a car. The head bartender was with her too."

Rob.

"Did you call the police?" Wilder barked.

Leo toed the sand. "I wanted to get to you first." No. He was protecting himself. Maybe his own daughter somehow. "Do you…do you think they'll kill her?"

"No," Shep and Wilder boomed. But loose ends were being cut.

Wilder clasped Shep's shoulder. "They have my sister."

As if Shepherd would let Wilder do this alone. He may have lost Caley and her love forever, but he wouldn't rest until he found her. He could at least make up for walking away by finishing this—like he'd wanted to all along. She *could* count on him.

"They might have taken her to the club," Shep said. Already they were hauling it to the parking lot.

"I'm going too," Leo said. "What if they have my daughter?"

"Fine." No time to argue. Caley was in danger. And he blamed himself. They climbed into Shep's rental car.

*God, please let her be at the club. Let us find her and keep her safe.* He'd never forgive himself for this. Never.

Would Caley?

# THIRTEEN

"No mercy," Shep said as they pulled into the alley at the Nest. The place would be in full swing. It was almost 2000 hours.

"No mercy," Wilder agreed.

Dr. Fines shouldn't have come with them. Palms rubbing on his thighs, continual licking of his lips. His fear would slow them down, but his daughter might be in danger and he loved her. "What does that mean?"

"It means whatever we gotta do to get answers and find Caley is what we're gonna do." Wilder chambered a 9mm into his Sig Sauer P226. "So I hope you don't have a weak stomach."

"If you do, then stay put," Shep added, removing his Sig from his ankle holster. "'Cause we're not gonna feel bad about it." He swung open the driver's-side door, Wilder right next to him, Leo bringing up the rear.

They strode straight to the bouncer guarding the back door. Shep pointed his gun at the bouncer's head. He went for his sidearm. "I wouldn't do that if I were you," Shep warned. "Where's Kyle Marx?"

Wilder aimed his gun on the bouncer, as well, surveying the alley at the same time. "My sister is missing. And this guy pointing a gun at your head. He's in love with her. So I'd think real smart and real fast about your answer."

Shep removed the gun from the goon's holster and shoved it in his waistband, keeping his gun trained between the man's eyes.

"He's not here."

"Where is he?" Shep demanded, sliding off the safety on his gun. "I'm not even gonna count."

"I don't know." Panic rose in his voice. "Rob said he's not coming in tonight." Bouncer's eyes darted from Wilder to Shep. "He has another business in Tampa. Sometimes he's there for several days."

"What kind of business? A club?"

"No." Sweat poured down his cheeks. "Exotic animals."

"Where in Tampa?" If they were taking Caley there, to Marx, then they had a thirty-minute head start already.

"I don't know, man. Never been. I just watch the door."

Yeah. Right. Shep put him out cold using pressure points before he could inhale another breath. Wilder dragged him behind the Dumpster and zip-tied his hands behind his back, then his feet.

Leo stood, mouth agape.

"You can stay out here or you can come with us, but we won't have time to save your hide if you get in a jam." Shepherd put his hand on the back door. "In or out, Fines?"

"I'm…I'm in. I'm in."

Shep nodded, surprised. Man had moxie. He'd give him that.

Inside the back area, two bouncers flanked the stairs leading to the offices. "I'll take the one on the left," Shepherd said.

Wilder grinned. "Nice of you to leave me the bigger guy."

Shep chuckled and they rushed the staircase.

"Hey! How'd you get in here?" said the goon on the right.

"I'm glad you asked," Wilder said and had him out

on the floor as fast as Shep took out the guy on the left. They dragged them under the staircase, zip-tied them and made haste upstairs. "Next time, give me more of a challenge. And there will be a next time, as I do not accept your resignation."

Shep had no choice. Wilder would have to get over it.

They sped down the hall to the office Caley had been held in once before.

A door opened and they trained their guns.

Billy Reynolds.

He glanced at Leo, at Shep. Recognition dawned and his eyes bugged out. He ran like a rabbit, taking a hard right. "This one's mine," Shep hollered as he bolted.

"Yeah, take the gangly kid," Wilder hollered back, but he didn't follow. He must have been heading into the office to find out the location of Kyle Marx's exotic animal business.

Shep yanked Billy by the scruff and pinned him against the wall, gun under his chin. "You been holing up here, Billy? I didn't know party-goers got to hang around in the offices." He kicked open an office door, dragging Billy inside. Leo stepped inside with him.

"Where's Darcy?" Leo demanded.

"I don't know!" Billy answered.

Shep slung him against the wall, not even trying to be delicate. Billy grunted.

"Where is Caley?"

Billy's face turned red. Shep loosened his forearm from Billy's throat and switched tactics, using the gun again. "Do I look like someone who plays games?"

Billy licked his lips. "No. No you don't. I don't know where she is. I promise."

"What happened to Mary Beth? And don't lie to me."

"It was an accident."

"What was an accident?"

Sweat poured down Billy's face. Shep switched off the safety making sure Billy heard the click. "One in the chamber with your name on it." He wouldn't kill him. But he would scare him half to death to get answers.

"We know about the turtle eggs you and Darcy dug up and brought here to the club. We know Mary Beth filmed it on her GoPro." Leo spoke with a calming voice. Professor-like.

"Did she call you out?" Shep asked.

"She thought I was cheating on her with Darcy. But I wasn't. So she followed me one night down to the beach and caught us poaching eggs."

"How could you?" Leo asked.

"The eggs. The turtles…the turtles paid big and I needed the college tuition." Billy's eyes reddened.

"Why did you kill her?"

"I didn't mean to. I wanted to make things right with her, so we met up at Palm Lake. But she wasn't there to get back with me. She told me she'd figured out the discrepancies in the turtle logs. She'd thought it might be Ashley or Toby, but after what she saw on the beach, she knew they weren't doing it. She threatened to go to you, Dr. Fines. And Caley. It would have ruined me. It got heated and she went to leave. I chased her down. And…it just happened. I freaked out. I didn't even know she was dead until she stopped kicking."

"Why didn't you take the GoPro?" Shep asked, disgust churning in his gut.

"I didn't know she had it with her. I thought she might have left it in her dorm, but you caught me before I could finish searching. So I checked Caley's house but you interrupted that too!"

As Shep suspected. He assumed Caley had found it. "You hurt an innocent old woman."

"That was an accident too!" Billy broke down, sobbing.

"I didn't want to stage Mary Beth's death. I loved her. But Darcy went to Kyle. We took Mary Beth. Darcy changed her into a swimsuit and we put her near the shore. Placed the kayak in the water. I didn't mean for it to happen."

But it did. "You did mean to attack Caley. That was no accident. And what about the oxygen tank? Did you do that?"

"No way. I wouldn't do that. Kyle knows a dive guy. I just…I just told him which tank was hers. He wanted her dead from the start. I had no control."

Shep squeezed Billy's shoulder, but refrained from doing what he'd like to do. Beat him within an inch of his life.

"Who attacked Caley on the beach?"

"One of Kyle's guys."

The door swung open and Shep aimed his gun.

Wilder.

Wilder glanced at Billy. "He know anything?"

"More than enough."

"I came up empty-handed. No address for the exotic animal business in Tampa."

Billy coughed, face reddening again. Shep eased up, giving him air. "I know where it's at. We've taken turtles there. I'll help you. Whatever you want." He rattled off the address to Shep while Wilder called Tom, revealing CliffsNotes-style what was going down and where he could come pick up the big baddies, including Billy Reynolds.

Shep pulled the same knockout number with Billy and left him in the closet for the police to detain. They didn't have time to stick around. "We need to haul it. Won't be long before someone realizes those guards aren't guarding anything. And we're almost an hour behind."

Wilder took the lead as they made their way down the

hall and back outside the club. Blue lights flashed in the distance.

Now to find Kyle Marx and rescue Caley.

The ride was the longest in history. They'd opted out of contacting Tampa's local PD for fear the sirens and lights might make Caley's abductors do desperate things. This needed to go down quietly and with the skill Shep and Wilder possessed, even if Shep couldn't help second-guessing the decision. The thirty-minute drive to Tampa was a long time.

Wilder kept a tight grip on the wheel, barely speaking. Shep's knee bounced like a drug addict needing a fix, his insides mimicking it. Neither brought up the fact that Shepherd had declared his love for Caley and quit.

Would she even care that he hadn't left? That he was doing everything in his power to save her?

They slowed at the street that led to a large exotic animal farm, masking what it really was. An illegal exotic animal ring. A front used to ship these creatures on the black market. Ship the eggs. Who knew what was inside?

"Leo, you should wait here," Shepherd said. "I don't know what we're getting into. You'll be safer in the car."

"My daughter might be inside. I'm going. I've made a lot of mistakes, but I want to make them right. I love my daughter. No matter what. I'd never forgive myself if something happened to her. And I know she's messed up. Horribly, but she's mine. And I can't stand by and do nothing."

"Fine," Wilder said.

This man had made some serious wrong calls lately, but his love for his daughter was pure. Unconditional. Maybe that's what God's fatherly love was also like. Pure. Unwavering. Because if anyone deserved to be punished it was Darcy Fines. And Shepherd. But Leo wasn't thinking about consequences right now. He just loved her.

A Psalm he'd skimmed in Caley's Bible came to his mind.
*Show me Your unfailing love in wonderful ways. By Your mighty power You rescue those who seek refuge from their enemies.*

Shepherd had made a lot of mistakes too. Looking back, God had rescued Shep. Time and again. Leading him all the way to Chaplain Chastain. To good friends like Wilder. And to Caley, who had shown him grace in so many ways, demonstrating it in a way he needed to see. From sandwiches to defending him before her brother.

But he'd annihilated it.

Could he make it right?

He'd hurt her more than anyone in his life.

Could he win her back?

Maybe not. But he could save her.

*God, help me right this. By Your mighty power rescue her. Rescue me from my past. Help me to truly surrender it all and let it go. Help me to believe. And give Caley the strength to show me grace again. To show me forgiveness.*

And if she didn't, he wouldn't blame her.

He'd disappear from her life. From Wilder's.

But he ached for grace.

They exited the car.

"We have about a half mile to the entrance," Wilder said. The facility was surrounded with fencing about twelve feet high and rolled in barbed wire. "I imagine there'll be security cameras there so we need to find a different entry point."

A large tin building sat about a click away. Adjacent to that was a small house. Where would Caley be?

"Pop the trunk," Wilder said. "Tom said he gave you some surveillance equipment and tools. I know you have them."

Shep popped the trunk and removed wire cutters. "Let's go in on the south side. We'll have better tree coverage." Wilder nodded and Shep took the lead, using a rabbit ears signal with his fingers to motion them to follow. He and Wilder sandwiched Leo as they kept to the shadows of the trees to gain entrance to the property.

"Ever used a gun, Leo?" Shep asked, retrieving his other ankle-holstered gun. A Glock.

"A few times. I'm not Rambo."

He might need a gun. This wasn't going to be an easy extraction. "You shoot. You shoot to kill. Understood?" Shep asked.

"No mercy," Leo echoed.

Shep wasn't one to not show mercy since God had shown him so much, but these guys weren't showing a drop. This wasn't about revenge or going in and taking out a group of human beings. It was dog eat dog. If Wilder and Shep didn't take them down, the other team wouldn't hesitate to kill them both and Leo…and Caley.

So… "No mercy."

Strapped to a chair, Caley surveyed her surroundings. Nothing but the stench of animals and their excrement. Stacked crates filled with animals lined the walls. Turtles, fish, birds, an array of cats. Lynx to tigers. Her heart tore in two.

Rob had brought her in and tied her up in an office with a glass window that looked into the immense warehouse. A sliding door led to a section beyond that. Who knew what was in there.

They seemed to have the larger animals sedated. They were too lethargic.

Burly Guy was standing outside. He'd been left to guard her. Where did Rob go? Would they stage her death too? First Mary Beth and now her.

*God, help me. Save me.*

What if He didn't? Then what?

She'd have to trust Him anyway. She didn't want to die. But knowing she'd be in the arms of Jesus if she did gave her some comfort.

Muffled voices sounded from the thin walls. Caley strained to listen.

"Why?" A woman's voice. "Please don't do this."

"I have no choice, Darcy." A man's voice. Not Rob. Not Burly Guy.

"No! No, don't!" The cries pinched Caley's heart. *Oh God!*

The crying slowly ebbed until there was nothing but silence. Caley's gut screamed Darcy was dead. She was going to be next.

She struggled with the ties, hoping to wiggle her way out. No go. The office door opened and Kyle Marx entered. "Caley Flynn. We finally meet. You've been a little pill."

"What did you do to Darcy?" she demanded, refusing to show fear.

"I'm afraid Darcy has always been in trouble with drugs and she's had an overdose." He feigned sadness, then grinned.

Anyone tied to this crazy animal ring was being picked off. "How many deaths can you fake before Turtle Bay police figure it out? Mary Beth. Darcy. Me? Did you kill Billy? He's missing." Everyone was turning up dead.

"He's safe. For today. Who knows? Maybe when summer is over and he goes back home, gets settled in school, he'll also have a tragic accident."

Caley struggled with her ties. She had to get out of here.

Kyle only laughed. "Caley, you should have never come into my club. Seen the eggs. You could have gotten off scot-free."

"The cops have the footage I took that night and the GoPro footage. They know your club is selling illegal turtle eggs. How are you going to get away with that?"

Kyle looked out the glass windows. "There won't be anyone to connect me to that. I'm so sorry this happened and in my own club. I'm appalled. Notice, I'm not on any of the videos."

Caley wanted to throw up.

"I might get a hefty fine but I can pay that." He sniffed. "Exotic animals aren't cheap."

"What about Leo? He'll know his daughter was murdered." Caley squeezed her eyes shut. Leo. Poor Leo.

"He might know it, but he won't be able to prove it. Besides, Leo won't say a word. He loves his job. And he gave me a nice stack of cash. Which I imagine can be traced to his bank account. If things go sideways, I always have a plan. Always."

Leo wouldn't roll over like that. Maybe he had for Mary Beth. And even Caley when she'd first been attacked. But not his own daughter.

"And what about me? No one will believe I killed myself. You think my brother or Shepherd Lightman will rest until they find you? Because they won't." She only hoped they'd rescue her in time. Except Shepherd was gone. On a plane. On a cruise. But Wilder would find her. He'd have to. "They'll take you apart limb by limb. Slowly. Painfully. I promise you that." Kyle didn't know Shepherd wouldn't be coming to save her.

"Feisty." He laughed. "No wonder Rob likes you so much." He ran his finger down her cheek. She jerked away. "Yes, feisty indeed. You remind me of an exotic animal. Backed against the wall."

"Doesn't she?" The door that had been cracked opened wider and in stepped Nora Simms.

"Nora?" Caley's brain wouldn't compute.

"Hello, Kyle. I got here as soon as I could. Had to give a stellar speech first." She turned to Caley. "Was that some applause or what?"

What was going on?

"You're in this together? You've been trafficking animals? Your dad would roll over in his grave!"

Nora's eyes slanted and she pointed a red-polished nail at Caley. "My father cared about nothing but those precious turtles. And when he died, he left his money to them. What did I get? A measly portion. So don't talk about my dad like he's a hero."

Caley shook her head. "This is some kind of sick revenge on your late father?"

Nora rolled her eyes. "This is about money, Caley. Money. And I don't mind kicking my dad when he's down." She laughed and pulled out a gun with a silencer.

She'd played them all.

"You think you and Kyle are going to just get away with this?"

Nora's smile turned sickeningly sweet. "This whole thing is a fiasco, Caley. Only one of us is getting out of it. And that's me." She aimed her gun and pulled the trigger.

Kyle Marx dropped dead on the floor.

Caley stared, unable to look away from the horrific sight. Blood pumped through her heart at wild speeds. Her ears rang.

"Everything points to Kyle and his club. But nothing points to me. This will look like nothing more than a thug club owner trying to sweep his mess under the rug with a very non-well-thought-out plan."

"And Leo?"

Nora frowned. "What about him? He might believe Darcy overdosed. He might believe Kyle killed her. Either way, what's that got to do with me?"

Leo would go on working for Nora Simms none the wiser.

Fear shot through her veins. With Kyle in control, Caley had had a chance. She might have been able to convince him that his plan had holes. That Shep was already on to him, and Wilder too.

But no one was on to Nora.

They'd think Kyle killed Caley. Case closed. They'd go home and grieve.

Nora would get away with it.

*Wait.* "You just killed your patsy. They'll know someone else is in on this."

Nora shook her head. "Not if they never find his body. They'll think he left the country. And I assure you, they won't find his body. And they won't find yours either."

So this was what hatred and greed looked liked.

Evil. Dark.

Striding to the door, Nora motioned for Burly Guy. "Take our guest to my most favorite creature. I'm leaving. Get rid of the bodies and evidence."

Burly Guy undid Caley's restraints. He and Rob manhandled her from the offices, through the warehouse of animals about to be sold and to a cage. He unlocked the padlocked door, and Caley's knees buckled.

She pressed into Rob. "Don't do this. You don't want to do this."

Caressing her cheek, he grinned. "I'm gonna miss that pretty face, *Meg*." He looked at Burly Guy. "But I'm not gonna watch. Come on."

Burly Guy shoved her inside and locked it. "Me neither."

Inside the large cage, a sleek Florida black panther stalked the perimeter.

Far from lethargic.

# FOURTEEN

Shep had used the wire cutters to create a crawl-through for them to enter the property. To the right of them was a large fenced-in area housing tigers. This could go really bad really fast. The warehouse lay straight ahead.

"Let's do a sweep of that house just to be sure," Wilder whispered.

Shep gnawed the inside of his lip. "No."

"What?"

"No." In their eyes Caley would be nothing but trouble. Causing all sorts of problems for them. They'd want to hurt her. Make her suffer. No better way than to force her to see animals—turtles—in caskets. Because that's how she'd see it. Like her grandfather. Right now she was probably reeling. "They'll have her out here."

"How do you know?"

"Because it'll inflict the most pain on Caley. Seeing those caged animals will be pure torture. They'll know that too. So the quicker we get in and get her away from that sight, the better."

Wilder rubbed his chin. "Shepherd, I've been off my rocker because of Meghan. Even if you hadn't already been in Florida, I would have sent you anyway."

Was that Wilder's way of apologizing?

"I'm protective because, to me, she is my *baby* sister.

I love her too, man. Forgive me for acting like a complete idiot?"

"This has nothing to do with my failed relationships? My past?"

"I wouldn't call what you had relationships, Shepherd." Wilder smirked. "I'm looking out for my sister. But if anyone is worthy of her, it's you, man. It's you. I don't care about your past. And Caley, sure as night is black, won't. Does she love you back?"

He wasn't sure now that he'd pushed her away. "I walked. Like I always do. I haven't changed."

"Not true. You walked away to protect her. Because you love her. Because you're afraid you might hurt her. It's stupid. And I should kick your butt for it, but I get it. And if you quit, then you're walking away from me too."

Wilder was right. He didn't want to leave. Before, with others, he'd been protecting himself. Getting out first, keeping them from abandoning him first. But not with Caley.

If anything he wanted to stay.

"I'm afraid it's too late." He'd messed up. Royally. She'd kicked him to the curb. By the time he found her, she wouldn't want him anymore. Like so many people before. He hadn't lived up to her expectations.

*A man who would leave me when I needed him most...*

But that wasn't going to stop him from rescuing her now.

"It's not too late. And you won't know until you ask her." Wilder used his hand and swiped it across the air as if opening a door. "So, brother," he said in that teasing tone he was famous for, "go get her. I'm right on your six."

"Me too," Leo said.

Wilder raised an eyebrow and pointed to Leo's gun. "Is that safety on?"

Leo glanced at the gun. "No."

"Then get in front of me."

Shepherd quietly laughed and scanned the building. One door on the north side. A double door on the south. They'd squeak. Metal. Drawing attention could get Caley killed if she wasn't already... No. He wouldn't go there. Couldn't live with the guilt if they'd made the wrong call to come alone.

A couple windows up on the second floor. He was sick to death of climbing into windows. "Going up and through to Grandma's house," he whispered, then darted to some trees near the building, Wilder and Leo following.

"I'll cover you from down here. Anyone comes out, they're going night-night. But if you're not out in ten minutes with her, I'm coming in."

"Roger that." Shep tucked his Sig in his waistband, pulled his knife from its sheath and clamped the blade between his teeth. He hoisted himself to the lowest branch and climbed his way up parallel with the window.

A branch stretched out giving him access to it, but he couldn't be sure it would hold. *God, let this thing hold.* Scooting out onto the branch, creaks and pops sent his heart slamming into his rib cage. This was his only shot.

Before the branch thinned into nothing but twigs, he laid his belly to the branch, shimmying until he could grasp the small window ledge. When he released his body from the branch he'd have to use his core and upper arm strength to keep himself from swinging into the building and announcing he was here.

Caley's life was at stake.

Hands on the window ledge, he dropped from the branch, moving toward impact on the metal building. Before he smacked into it, he used all the power he had to stop his body an inch from the building. He lifted himself up, eye level with the window. Shep used one hand to keep his body upright and the other to push on the window.

If it didn't open… It did!

Sliding the window open, he hauled himself inside. Sweat trickled down his back and temples. He was in a loft that overlooked… Heart jumping into his throat, Shep watched as a sleek black panther stalked Caley.

She eased backward, hands out in front of her. She tripped over her long red dress.

Shep pulled his gun, aimed between the metal bars…

The situation was dire. The animal needed to be put down and he had the shot. But Caley wouldn't want this.

He quickly scanned the loft. No time to go down there. No time to look for a… Gun!

Shep spied a tranquilizer gun. Keeping his gun trained on the panther, he quickly but quietly secured the rifle. Darts lay in an open velvet-lined box. He grabbed them, chambered four and slid to the edge of the loft floor, belly down.

The panther growled at an ear-piercing level.

Caley shook uncontrollably, tripping on her dress again. She landed near a large log and snatched it.

This was not how it was going to end. Not if Shep had his way.

The panther charged.

As it lunged for her, fangs bared, huge paws splayed, she raised the branch as a pitiful barrier.

Shep pulled the trigger.

Twice.

The muscled animal landed on top of her, knocking her to the ground with a thud.

He raced down the loft stairs as she shoved the panther off, eyes wide, still shaking. She was in shock. Her dress was tattered at the hem.

She swiveled in his direction.

Made eye contact.

His heart lurched, but he moved toward her. Wilder

would be coming through the door soon if he didn't get her out, and he wasn't sure how many men were in the building.

He made his way to the cage. Her lips trembled as they spoke his name. "Shepherd. I thought…you left me."

He never should have.

He rested the rifle against the cage, his own hands shaking. "Are you hurt?" If they laid a finger on her…

"No. Why are you here? Where's my brother?"

She didn't want him. She wanted Wilder. As he expected. He'd destroyed the one good thing in his life. He clasped her hands, which were holding the bars of the cage, fear clinging to his tongue. "He's outside but probably not for long. Let me get you out of here."

"Fine." Her tone sounded clipped. She had every right to be angry, but that didn't stop the splinters burrowing into his chest.

Dozens upon dozens of crated animals were going nuts in protest. The eruption of screeches, barks, meows and roars were enough to cause a person to go mad. This must be killing Caley. He'd make sure they were freed. ASAP.

Shepherd eyed the padlock. He could pick it but he needed… Her hair was still pulled off to the side, baring one of her delicate shoulders.

He swallowed and reached through the bars, sliding his hand into her satiny hair. The look in her eyes sent wildfire through his veins. Her hair fell loose as he retrieved the pin. "Where are the others?"

"Kyle's dead. Nora Simms is in charge of it all, but she left." Caley pointed to the other side of the building. "Offices are over there. Rob is here, but he's not the one who shot at me like we guessed. One of the bouncers from the club has a sling on his arm. There might be one or two more here, as well."

Shep grunted and glanced at the panther again. "How long will those tranquilizers keep that animal down?"

Studying the panther Caley scratched her head. "Depends on what the sedative is. Fentanyl. Telazol. But thirty minutes to an hour."

"Who locked you in here?" he asked as he worked on the lock. The idea of someone doing something so vile heated him to the boiling point.

"Rob and the burly guy from the alley."

"I'll deal with them in a minute." The lock clicked and Shep removed the padlock.

A metal screech blended in with the animal noises and Wilder entered the warehouse. He pointed to the offices upstairs. Shep held up five fingers. He nodded and headed for the stairs, Leo behind him.

"Darcy's dead," Caley whispered. "Kyle staged an overdose. Before Nora killed him point-blank." She glanced at the stairs leading to the offices. "You should go help Wilder. He could get hurt. And Leo too."

Shepherd smirked. "You must not know your brother well. They won't know what hit them. He's that fast. That silent. Leo will be safe." He handed her back the pin. "It's time for you to go, Little Flynn. Get to safety."

She stepped out of the cage. "Shepherd, why are you here then? If he's that good. If he can keep me safe like you said."

He should muster some courage. Lay it out like she had earlier. But he wanted her to be safe first. "Caley, I don't expect you to understand." The animals went even wilder. Shep shoved her back into the cage. "Get down!"

"Shep!"

"Hands up, tough guy." Nora Simms stood twenty feet away, gun in hand. Guess she'd come back or never left after all. "I can't leave here with the both of you knowing the truth. Drop your weapons and kick them across the floor."

"Don't do it, Shep!" Caley hollered.

Nora trained her gun on Caley. "You want to watch her die first? Weapons. Now."

Shepherd retrieved two guns and a knife, kicking them across the floor with a clatter while he contemplated the scenarios to free them.

Nora must not realize Wilder and Leo were inside.

She fired.

Heat seared through Shep's upper torso, knocking him off-kilter. He bit back the pain. Anger rising. The crazy broad wasn't going to get another shot at him.

"Shep!" Caley cried.

Nora stomped toward Shep. *That's right. Keep your focus off her.*

"You don't want to do this, Nora," Caley pleaded.

"Yes," she hissed, venom in her eyes. "I do."

Shep spread his arms wide. "Well, come on then," he taunted her. If Nora ignored Caley, she'd have a chance to run, which would give Nora pause and he'd disarm her. So maybe he would let her get another shot. Whatever it took to keep Caley unharmed, to let her know how much she meant to him. Everything. She was the light in all his dark places. The hope to his despair. His heart.

He'd take an arsenal of bullets to show her.

"I'm not sure if you're stupid or brave." Nora aimed the gun at his head.

Caley slipped the tranquilizer gun through the bars.

She was supposed to be running for it!

"I'm probably a bit of both."

The gun knocked against the metal. The noise interrupted Nora. She swung around, aiming for Caley. Shep lunged for her, grabbing her arm. Nora fired.

Caley fired too.

Sparks flew from the metal bars. Nora's shot missed; her gun crashed on the concrete floor and she collapsed. Shep shoved her gun in his waistband, his upper left shoulder on fire, blood seeping through his shirt, coating his skin.

Caley raced to Shepherd. "How bad is it?"

"Through and through. I'll live. Good shot, Little Flynn."

"I'm navy trained."

Could he love this woman any more? "Mmm…" Shepherd chuckled.

Sirens wailed in the distance.

Wilder blew into the room, pausing and scanning the cage, the sleeping panther and sleeping Nora. He focused on Shep, narrowed his eyes. Shep gave him the okay sign and Wilder visibly relaxed.

"Leo?" Caley asked.

Wilder's lips turned south. "He's upstairs. Didn't want to leave his daughter."

Not even in death. The way it should be when you loved someone. Like he was learning how God loved him. He was a son. There was no tossing him back to foster care. God had signed the dotted line in blood.

Now if only Caley could show him the same grace she'd shown him countless times before. Offer him some mercy. He'd beg if necessary. He'd never begged for anything. Not even when he was being punished without dinner and starving. But he'd do it for this woman. He didn't realize how empty and hungry he'd been until he stepped into her world.

A world that he wanted to be a part of. For life.

"Caley…" he whispered.

She stared at Wilder. "And the men from the club? Are they…? Did you…?"

"All secured in a neat pretty row awaiting the authorities." Wilder pointed to Shep's wound and looked at Caley with that stupid grin. "You do that to him for being an idiot earlier today?"

She finally turned to him, held his gaze, a mix of confusion and hope in her eyes. "How were you an idiot? Other than trying to fall on your sword for me just now."

"You were supposed to run. Not shoot." He was angry and frustrated and he wanted to yank her against him and kiss the mess out of her. But his shoulder hurt like crazy and Wilder was standing about fifteen feet back.

"As if I'd have run and left you alone," she said.

He stroked her cheek. "No," he murmured. "You're not a runner. You don't leave. That's what I do."

She swallowed. "But you came back for me." Her lip trembled. "Why?"

He cupped her neck. "I died standing there today watching you hurt and knowing I'd caused it. I told you I wasn't good. But you make me want to be. You make me want to stay. I never wanted to leave."

She shook her head, confusion in her eyes. "Why did you then?"

"For so long I've been closed off. I lost hope of being loved a long time ago. But you did something to me, Caley. You found a way inside those locked vaults. You gave me hope again. If I've ever seen what love is, I've seen it in you, Caley Flynn."

Tears pooled in her eyes.

"I walked away for fear I'd mess up. I was terrified you'd see how unworthy I am of your love and that when you did…" He bit the inside of his quivering lip and waited a beat to compose his shaky voice. "When you did, you'd leave me. And that's something I wouldn't recover from."

Wilder groaned. "If this is about to turn into a moment that might scar a brother's eyes, I'm gonna wait outside for the blue and paramedics to get here." He glanced at the cage and strode over, locking the door. "Just in case *Bagheera* wakes up early and wants a kiss too." He winked and jogged out the side door.

Shepherd ran his hand through her hair. "I don't deserve forgiveness, but I'm asking." He dropped to his knees and wrapped his arms around her waist. "Because I love you, Caley Flynn." Burrowing into the folds of her dress, he embraced her, smelled the perfume that was her signature scent. He felt her hands work through his hair.

"Shepherd Lightman, what did you just say?"

He peered up into her eyes. "I love you. I've never said that to anyone in my whole life."

Caley clutched his cheeks and knelt; tears slipped down her face. "We all make mistakes. I'm going to make them too. I already have. I shouldn't have thrown your past in your face. I promise to never do that again. Because I love you. I love everything about you. From your terrible comforting skills to the fierce soldier who's bleeding on my behalf without so much as a flinch. I forgive you," she whispered. "Forgive me."

This woman undid him. Loved him even when he'd crushed her to the core. He couldn't explain it and couldn't let it slip away. Not ever. "You're forgiven. Now—" he grinned "—kiss me. I need some physical contact." He guided her to him.

Feather soft at first.

Building with raw emotion.

Heady. Intense.

Reeling at the tender grace she offered even in a kiss.

She tasted like goodness and hope.

It mounted with passion.

With promise.

To make it past three weeks.

To soar straight into forever.

# EPILOGUE

*November*

Caley sat on the beach in Okinawa, the waves rolling in and teasing her bare toes before darting off into the depths. After the incident at the exotic animal farm—a front for trafficking exotic animals—Nora Simms had been arrested for illegal animal trading, murder and attempted murder. The animals had been properly placed in rehabilitation centers. Billy Reynolds and the goons and bartender from the club had been arrested, as well.

Leo Fines had mourned his daughter and buried her. Caley had attended the service with Shepherd at her side. In a sling. He was right. His wound had been a clean through and through. Stitches. Antibiotics.

Miss Whittle was right about the deep waters. About trusting God even when it hurt. When it didn't make sense. When answers didn't come in the way she expected. Shepherd had come back. For her. And Miss Whittle's son was moving to Turtle Bay. They both got to be with the ones they loved.

Which made it easier for Caley to leave.

With the grant secured and donors willing to give, even after hearing about Nora Simms's involvement, Caley saw her interns off in the fall and shared the turtle crawl with Shep. They'd watched as hundreds upon hundreds of hatchlings emerged from their shells and made their way to sea, home, led by the moonlight. And God had led Caley and Shepherd to each other. That night, Shepherd had proposed on the sandy shore—Caley's favorite place in the world. No longer one of fear, but of happiness. Of love. She'd now been married to the man of her dreams for four whole days. It had been a beach wedding right outside her Florida bungalow. Best four days of her life so far. Because she was indeed living. No more hiding in a protective shell. For as long as she had this man, she'd love him. Heart and soul. She'd live well and love well.

"What are you doing out here?" Shepherd padded down the private beach in a pair of basketball shorts. He plopped next to Caley and pulled her onto his lap. She wrapped her arms around his neck, his dress shirtsleeves hanging over her fingers, but she loved it. Loved wearing it. Loved having his smell so close.

They'd flown into Okinawa the morning after their wedding. Wilder had owed Shep a cruise. They got a honeymoon at his expense instead, and Caley had dreamed of a honeymoon where she could swim with sea turtles.

"Listening to the waves, watching the tide roll in. Thinking about you."

"Yeah?" He nipped her bottom lip. "Good thoughts?"

"Mmm…the best." She toyed with the hair at the base of his neck.

He drew back, looked into her eyes. "Are you sure you want to leave Turtle Bay? I meant it when I said I'd move. Find a job close by."

They'd batted that back and forth since he'd proposed. If Caley wanted him to be safe, he'd do something safer. Wilder had protested. But Caley was okay with who Shepherd was. She didn't want him to be anyone else.

She framed his face. "I love the Atlanta Aquarium. I

don't need the beach out my back door. I just need you. And I'm truly okay with the dangers of your job."

Leo Fines had made up for his failure to care earlier on. He'd been a brave man, going into the line of fire with Shep and Wilder. And he'd used his contacts to get Caley a job at the Atlanta Aquarium as one of their sea turtle marine life vets.

"And I need you to be happy."

"I am happy, Shepherd. *You* make me happy." She kissed him lightly on the lips, on each scruffy cheek.

"We'll buy a house."

"I like your loft in downtown Atlanta. It's cozy and, well, it needs better decor but for the most part, I love it. I love you. Now hush and lay some physical contact on me." His comforting skills had improved 1000 percent. Because he was free to love and be loved without the fear of abandonment. "I love you. Always."

"Always," he echoed as he slipped her glasses from her face and claimed her lips.

Gentle yet powerful.

Strategic yet lazy.

Like their first kiss.

As if every kiss would be a first kiss.

Until death did them part.

\* \* \* \* \*

*If you liked this story from Jessica R. Patch,
check out her other Love Inspired Suspense titles:*

**FATAL REUNION
PROTECTIVE DUTY
CONCEALED IDENTITY
FINAL VERDICT**

*Available now from Love Inspired!*

*Find more great reads at www.Harlequin.com*

Dear Reader,

I think sometimes we believe that when we mess up, God will withhold His love from us. We compare a perfect God to imperfect people. People can disappoint us, hurt us, abandon us and leave us a shredded mess. Sometimes on purpose. Sometimes not. But God never changes His mind about us. He loves us no matter how many times we mess up. He loves us unconditionally. Wholly. He never withholds His love. His arms are always open.

I'm glad Shepherd learned that. My prayer is that if you've felt this way, you'll let God prove you wrong. He wants to lavish you with love, mercy and grace. You belong to Him. Always.

I'd love to hear from you. Connect with me at jessica@jessicarpatch.com and stay "Patched In" by joining my email list at www.jessicarpatch.com.

Warmly,
*Jessica*

## COMING NEXT MONTH FROM
# Love Inspired® Suspense

### Available August 8, 2017

## BODYGUARD
*Classified K-9 Unit* • by Shirlee McCoy
The last assignment FBI agent Ian Slade wants is guarding Esme Dupree, a member of the crime family responsible for his parents' deaths. But since she's the key witness in her brother's murder trial, her family wants her dead... and it's Ian's and his faithful K-9 partner's jobs to keep her alive.

## PLAIN RETRIBUTION
*Amish Country Justice* • by Dana R. Lynn
When Rebecca Miller, a deaf woman who left her Amish community years ago, is stalked by a criminal connected to her past, she needs help. The only local police officer who knows sign language is Miles Olsen, and he's determined to protect her.

## HOMEFRONT DEFENDERS
*Secret Service Agents* • by Lisa Phillips
Arriving in Hawaii on the advance team preparing for a presidential visit, Secret Service agent Alana Preston and director James Locke uncover plans for a possible assassination attempt. And the conspirators are dead set on killing anyone who gets between them and the commander-in-chief.

## MISSION UNDERCOVER
*Rangers Under Fire* • by Virginia Vaughan
His cover blown, police officer Blake Michaels is shot and left for dead. Now he has only one ally—Holly Mathis, a nurse who has evidence of a corrupt officer's wrongdoing. But in a town where everyone's loyalty is suspect, who can they trust?

## QUEST FOR JUSTICE
by Kathleen Tailer
After Bailey Cox's private investigator father is murdered, she works with Detective Franklin Kennedy—the policeman who once arrested her—to uncover the secret her father was investigating and to track down his killer. But as they come closer to the truth, they become the killer's next targets.

## DEADLY DISCLOSURE
by Meghan Carver
When law student Hannah McClaron is shot at on her way to work, FBI agent Derek Chambers rescues her...then reveals she's adopted and in danger from her mafia birth family. Can he keep her safe long enough to unravel the mystery of her past?

---